TRIPLE THREAT

Also by Jacqueline Guest in
the Lorimer Sports Stories series

TRIPLE THREAT

Jacqueline Guest

James Lorimer & Company Ltd., Publishers
Toronto

James Lorimer & Company Ltd., Publishers acknowledges the support of the Ontario Arts Council. We acknowledge the financial support of the Government of Canada through the Canada Book Fund for our publishing activities. We acknowledge the support of the Canada Council for the Arts for our publishing program. We acknowledge the Government of Ontario through the Ontario Media Development Corporation's Ontario Book Initiative.

Cover Image: iStockphoto

The Canada Council | Le Conseil des Arts
for the Arts | du Canada

ONTARIO ARTS COUNCIL
CONSEIL DES ARTS DE L'ONTARIO

MIX
Paper from
responsible sources
www.fsc.org   FSC® C016245

Library and Archives Canada Cataloguing in Publication

Guest, Jacqueline
        Triple threat / Jacqueline Guest.

(Sports stories)
Issued also in electronic format.
ISBN 978-1-55277-690-2

        I. Title. II. Series: Sports stories (Toronto, Ont.)

PS8563.U365T74 2011   jC813'.54   C2010-906634-0

James Lorimer & Company Ltd.,   Distributed in the United States by:
Publishers   Orca Book Publishers
317 Adelaide St. West   P.O. Box 468
Suite #1002   Custer, WA USA
Toronto, ON Canada   98240-0468
M5V 1P9
www.lorimer.ca

Printed and bound in Canada.
Manufactured by Friesens Corporation in Altona, Manitoba, Canada in June 2011.
Job #66709

For my very special daughters, Vanessa and Kristina —
thank you for showing me the world is in a dewdrop
and there are diamonds in the snow.

CONTENTS

1 GUESS WHO'S COMING TO VISIT?

"Mom, I'm home!" Matt Eagletail called as he walked in the door. It led to the basement family room of the spacious new house. Matt's room was also on this lower level, away from the rest of the family, and he loved the privacy it gave him. He still hadn't adjusted completely to his new life.

It had been just a few months since his mom, Colleen Eagletail, an absolutely great First Nations lady, had married Gordon Thoreau, an okay — but really white — guy, and Matt's universe had been turned up-side down. Not only had he acquired a new stepdad, but also an entire crowd of five unbelievable stepsisters! Two sets of twins aged six and eight, who made life interesting, to put it mildly, and a twelve-year-old step-sister, who started out irritating but became outright exasperating when you got to know her.

As Matt walked past his bedroom, he threw down his pack. He wouldn't be needing it for a while. As he passed by, he noticed his room was getting out of control again. It was still possible to see what colour his carpet was, but it wouldn't take much before the entire floor was hidden under his discarded clothing. He'd have to take five and clean it up one of these days before his mom went ballistic.

But not today. Today was the last day of school and summer holidays stretched out ahead like some exotic land waiting to be explored. Matt continued into the family room where the most important piece of equipment in the entire house sat quietly humming in the corner — the computer. He sat down at the desk and pressed the button to bring the machine to life. Once the screen lit up, he moved the cursor over the Internet icon and clicked *Connect*. Then he ran upstairs to quickly grab an after-school snack.

The Bragg Creek Bandits, the school basketball team he played for, had taken on the Millarville Mavericks for an end-of-school game, and Matt, who played point guard, was ravenous from the strenuous workout. He loved the game and always gave a hundred and ten percent.

The house seemed unusually quiet to Matt, which was odd for this time of day. The note on the kitchen table was from his mom.

Hi, Honey Bear!
You forgot I'm picking up both sets of twins and we're going out for ice cream to celebrate the end of school or the start of holidays, I can't remember which. This

means you and Jazz will have to find your own milk and cookies.
Love, Mom.
P.S. Jazz — I told you he'd forget about everything!

His mom had been right — he had forgotten. At the mention of Jasmine, the oldest of his new stepsisters, Matt winced. Jazz had told him the twins were being picked up, but it had slipped his mind. Whoops. As the oldest, it was one of his new responsibilities to make sure the *Geese* — that is, his little stepsisters — were either on the school bus or walking the two kilometres home with Jazz or himself. This was the first time he'd screwed up. It was a good thing his mom had picked the girls up or he'd have never heard the end of it.

"Matt, you loser!" A door slammed in the basement.

There was no mistaking that voice. It was Jazz. Then the other part of what he'd forgotten sprang into his brain. He was supposed to meet Jazz after the basketball game at school and walk home with her. This was bad.

Moving quickly, Matt pulled two glasses out of the cupboard. Grabbing the milk from the refrigerator with one hand, he used the other to reach for the fresh banana bread his mom had left. Carrying everything to the huge table where the family ate, Matt poured milk in the glasses, grabbed a knife out of a drawer, and was cutting two huge pieces when Jazz came storming into the kitchen.

"You didn't wait for me after the game, you jerk! I

had to look all over the dumb school for you and you weren't even there! If Precious hadn't told me he saw you on the trail as he was coming to meet me, I might still be waiting at the school." Jazz stopped her tirade when she saw what Matt was preparing.

"Sorry, Jazz. It slipped my greasy little mind." Then her words registered. *Precious* had told her he'd left? Hmm. Precious was Jazz's dog, a very large Great Pyrenees. Matt looked behind Jazz to where the big white dog silently stood near enough to his master to help if she needed him.

"Tattletale," he said to the hairy mutt, and then turned back to Jazz. "I made you a snack." He proudly held out a slab of banana bread.

"You made *yourself* a snack, Hotshot, and added me on after you remembered you'd left me dangling at school." She looked at him knowingly, her face still frowning. Then, with a toss of her long blond ponytail, she shrugged her slim shoulders and reached for the snack. "But since you're trying to be a nice guy, I accept your apology *and* your banana bread. I see you already have the computer fired up. Tell Free Throw we're all looking forward to his visit." She rummaged in her backpack and pulled out a copy of a teen magazine, then sat down to eat.

"I will," Matt called over his shoulder as he grabbed his own goodies and headed back downstairs. At the mention of Free Throw — the screen name of his best friend — the excitement that had been building for the last couple of weeks bubbled up inside of him. He'd met Free Throw in a chat room on the Internet, where they immediately hit it off when they'd discovered they shared a passion for basketball. In fact, they both planned to go on to careers in the NBA when they finished school.

Setting the milk and bread down, he sat in front of the computer and quickly went through the steps that would take him to the basketball chat room where he and Free Throw always met.

He signed in using his own screen name: Point Guard.

Point Guard: Is there a future NBA coach by the name of Free Throw just waiting to chat with a future rookie-of the-year point guard such as myself?

Matt watched as dialogue from other people in the chat room scrolled up the screen. Then suddenly, a message from Free Throw winked up on the monitor.

Free Throw: Hello up there in the frozen North. How are things? Down here in sunny San Francisco, it's a balmy eighty-two degrees — that's Fahrenheit, Buddy, not that crazy system you Canucks use!

Matt grinned as he began typing in his message.

Point Guard: Let's PM so we can discuss important

plans without a thousand interested parties joining in.

The plans they were going to discuss were the preparations for Free Throw's upcoming visit to Bragg Creek, which was scheduled to happen in less than a week. Once they were chatting to each other in private messaging mode, Matt told Free Throw about today's game, which the Bandits had won, and how much he was looking forward to his friend's visit.

Free Throw: Not half as much as me, old buddy. This will be the first time I've gone so far from home without the folks and my mom is driving me crazy. She's already had me to the doc twice to make sure I can make this trip.

Matt wondered what Free Throw meant for a second, and then realized what he was talking about. Several years ago, Free Throw had been in a car accident and, because his spinal cord had been damaged, he was paralyzed from the waist down. He had to use a wheelchair to get around. Travelling and being away from his own home would be a little trickier for someone who couldn't walk. Matt knew from personal experience moms could be really smothering sometimes, even when everything worked. Free Throw's mom must be over the edge.

Point Guard: It won't be long now. My stepdad has already bought the lumber to build a ramp so you can get in upstairs. I don't think you'll have any trouble with most of the stuff because I'm all set up down here, complete with a bathroom.

Free Throw: Your family is great. I'm sure we can muddle through. I'm pretty much the same as you, except I have a little trouble with that first step.

Point Guard: You're not the only one. So far three out of four twins have fallen down the narrow back stairs we all use to get to the lower floor and Mom is thinking of making the girls go around to the outside door so they won't have to negotiate the tricky part. Geese! Maybe they need training wheels, or rubber bumpers.

Matt still had to remind himself that Free Throw was in a wheelchair. It was hard to treat someone different when they seemed so *normal*. Maybe that was it. Free Throw *was* normal, he simply couldn't walk. Matt always felt bad when he made a mistake and said things like "We'll go for a walk when you get here," or used expressions such as "Stand up for yourself." Free Throw had told him not to worry. In fact, he'd told Matt he preferred it when people were themselves around him and didn't creep him out by treating him like he had some exotic disease.

They talked about the schedule of things they were going to do when Free Throw got there and, of course, the latest news from the NBA. Eventually, the two boys were talked out. Matt was sure everything would be great and Free Throw said he didn't care what happened once he arrived. It would all be part of the experience of living with a real, honest-to-goodness Canadian family.

Matt signed off, shaking his head. If Free Throw wanted the experience of living with a Canadian family, then he'd better tighten his seat belt, because he doubted any family was like his.

★ ★ ★

Supper was always a noisy time at Matt's house. Somehow everyone had an opinion and no one was shy about expressing it.

"And I've got a plumber coming over to customize your shower so Free Throw can use it with no problem," Matt's stepdad said, reaching for the bowl of baby carrots.

"Will Free Throw go right in the shower in his wheelchair, Matty?" Marigold, his six-year-old stepsister, asked as she carefully built several separate mounds out of her mashed potatoes.

"I don't know, Goldie. You'll have to ask him." Matt watched, fascinated, as his youngest stepsister dealt with her supper. Her small, freckled face was screwed up in concentration as she worked at the food on her plate.

After she'd separated the potatoes, she took the

rest of her vegetables and built potato snowmen. They had peas for eyes and the traditional baby carrot for a nose with a carefully placed French bean for a mouth. Sometimes the mouth curved up and sometimes down depending on whether the potato people were happy or sad. How this was determined, only Marigold knew for sure. Her bright, shining eyes twinkled as she decided this particular collection of vegetable people were all going to be very happy indeed. After that was done, she placed a small piece of meat by one potato person and a tidy pile of corn by another. Matt's eyebrows drew together in puzzlement.

Marigold saw him frowning. She shook her head, sending her curly red hair flying about her face like a fringe of fire. "Can't you see what they're doing, Matty?" she asked him,

"Uh, actually, Goldie, I can't," he said, still looking at the meat and corn.

Marigold rolled her eyes and sighed loudly. "This potato daddy is going to make a steak barbecue for his family because he loves them very much and wants them to eat meat so they'll grow up big and strong like him," she said, indicating the small piece of meat beside the mushy figure. "And this," she pointed at the potato snowman next to the corn, "is a potato pirate and that's his Jolly Roger gold that he stole from the King of the Veggies." Once her dinner diorama was complete, Marigold eagerly munched her way through the vegetable villagers, beginning with the pirate. Matt could only shake his head.

Gordon and his mom had given up telling the girls not to play with their food. His mom had decided it was more important that the girls eat their vegetables than worry if their manners were perfect. That would come later.

Marigold's performance seemed a little odd, until you watched her sister Daisy eat. Daisy wouldn't let any of her food touch and insisted on wiping her fork off between different foods. When she drank, she always turned the glass so she had a nice clean spot to drink from each time.

She had informed Matt that the reason for doing this was simple. The little man in her stomach, who looked after her supper once she swallowed it, found it easier to put each of the foods in its own compartment if she ate that way. Matt had declined to argue with this logic, especially after his stepsister had then told him the best part about the little man: It seemed no matter how much you ate, he always had a secret trap door to a dessert compartment where there was ample storage for the biggest piece of chocolate cake.

As if that wasn't enough, Violet and Rosemary, the eight-year-olds, had only yesterday decided they weren't going to eat anything that could talk back. Matt was still trying to figure that one out. Usually these twins were very serious and at times even thoughtful, but not at mealtime.

He watched as Violet, her voice very serious,

addressed her pork chop, and then waited. She watched intently, her lively brown eyes focused on her plate. Apparently pork chops did have opinions since Violet nodded her head in agreement, then took her fork and proceeded to transfer the talkative piece of meat to Matt's plate. Hey, this was one bizarre little girl thing that he could go along with!

Yeah, Free Throw was going to love this average Canadian family.

"Matt, did you hear about the R-M-S-B-L?" Jazz asked between mouthfuls.

Matt looked at her blankly. "And that would be . . ."

Jazz stared at him, shocked at his ignorance. "Matthew Eagletail-Thoreau, you've got to be joking! The RMSBL is only the hottest ticket for the summer around here. Didn't they keep up on important things like the RMSBL when you lived on the reserve?" she asked.

Before the big family merger, Matt and his mom had lived on the Tsuu T'ina reserve, which was adjacent to Bragg Creek. They had lived with his grandparents and, even now, Matt sometimes had pangs of homesickness, especially when he thought of his old basketball team, the Tsuu T'ina Warriors. He glanced over at Jazz, who was smiling smugly.

Matt could feel himself getting angry with his know-it-all sister. "If you don't stop with the alphabet soup I'm not going to talk to you at all, Jasmine

Eagletail-Thoreau." He gave her a look that should have turned her to stone. It didn't. She kept on talking.

"FYI, Matt — that's *for your information*, in case you can't figure that one out either — the RMSBL is the *Rocky Mountain Summer Basketball League*, and it's only the greatest invention since the music video." She smiled at him, and then let her jaw drop so he could see her mouth full of partially chewed food.

"Nice, Jazz. Did you learn that one while you were staying at the zoo or is it a natural talent?" he shot back.

"That's enough, you two. There are young ladies at the table." Matt's mom said, silencing Jazz before she had a chance to fire another zinger back at him.

"It sounds interesting, Jazz. Tell us more about it," Gordon Thoreau said, rescuing Rosemary's pork chop before it reached Precious's under-the-table disposal service.

"Well," Jazz began, looking around the table to make sure her entire audience was paying attention. "The League was formed so that kids who are into basketball wouldn't have to wait two whole months before they could play again. After all, basketball isn't something that you shelve just because it's summer." She took another big bite and swallowed without chewing.

"The way it works is, a team of no more than ten players signs up. This team competes against all the other teams, with each win counting as two points, then, when all the teams have competed against each other, the top eight square off in a round robin tournament to decide the grand winner."

"Sounds great." Matt's stepdad enthused.

Matt tried to look like he wasn't interested, so the Queen of Annoying didn't think she'd scored too many points.

"But you haven't heard the best part." she went on. "The final winner gets an awesome prize. Each player on the team gets a new pair of top-rated court shoes, personalized with his team number on them, and," she paused again, "an autographed jersey from their fave NBA player!" Jazz sat back and belched loudly.

"Jasmine! Excuse yourself," Colleen Eagletail-Thoreau admonished her new stepdaughter.

Matt hid a mischievous smile. "Yeah, Jazz. There are young ladies at the table."

Jazz grinned broadly at him. "What do you think?"

"I'd say about six point five on the Richter scale. Not bad for a girl." He nodded appreciatively.

"No, Hotshot." Jazz rolled her eyes. "I mean about the league. Are you going to get a team together and join? It would be a lot of fun."

Matt thought about this. He'd *really* like to play basketball over the summer. You couldn't take a chance on losing your edge. But Free Throw was coming. How would he feel about watching a bunch of guys play ball when he couldn't?

Matt's mom saw his hesitation. "Are you worried about Free Throw?"

Matt was sure his mom was telepathic. No one could guess right about stuff as often as she did.

"I don't want him to feel . . . left out." He hoped her telepathy would fill in the blanks. He didn't want to hurt his friend's feelings, but man, would he ever like to play b-ball over the summer.

"Why would he be left out? I thought you said Free Throw planned on a coaching career in the NBA. Isn't this a good place to start?" Colleen smiled at her son. "He'll arrive in less than a week. You could ask him when he gets here. I think you two are good enough friends that he'd give you a straight answer."

Matt thought about this. It wouldn't hurt to ask. In the meantime, he'd start thinking of guys who would want to play — if Matt and Free Throw decided to form a team, that is. And that was exactly what it would take — both of them, together. The minute Free Throw stepped off that plane, Matt was going to talk to him man-to-man, or at least guy-to-guy.

He smiled at his mom as she began serving a beautiful chocolate strawberry mousse for dessert. It was a new recipe and she wanted to try it out on her toughest critics before she offered it to her clients. His mom had her own successful catering company and some of Matt's fondest childhood memories involved sampling his mother's desserts.

As he reached for a big bowl, Matt already had a good feeling that everything was going to work out great.

2 EVERY TEAM STARTS WITH SOME PROBLEMS

Today was the day! Matt and his stepdad watched the screen announcing the arrival of various flights at the Calgary International Airport. Suddenly the screen blinked, showing that Free Throw's plane had landed. Matt waited impatiently. Then the automatic doors opened and there he was.

Hesitantly, Matt walked toward his friend. The boy in the wheelchair had sandy brown hair, clear hazel eyes, and his obviously well-muscled shoulders contrasted with Matt's slight build.

When Free Throw saw Matt, he wheeled his chair toward him. "Point Guard?" he asked tentatively.

Matt felt a little awkward. He wasn't sure what he should say.

Then the stranger in the wheelchair grinned. "What? I'm even more handsome than you expected?"

Matt smiled. "Yeah, that's it. In fact, you're too handsome for words, old buddy." He instantly relaxed. Free Throw sounded the same in person as he did on the Internet. "The truth is, I just can't get over that coat you're wearing." He nodded at the Toronto Raptors jacket Free Throw had draped around his shoulders.

"Oh, this old thing?" Free Throw raised his eyebrows in surprise. "What, you don't like this great Canadian team? I had no idea!" He waited for Matt's reaction. A smile tugged at the corners of Free Throw's mouth as understanding dawned on his friend's face.

"You brought that for Jazz, didn't you? I'd forgotten I'd told you she's the only Raptors fan in the house."

Free Throw grinned. "Hey, if your sister is as good as you say, we should encourage her. The sport could use more quality female players."

"She really is awesome, but don't tell Jazz I said she's good. I have enough trouble living with her now without having her ego get any bigger." Matt suddenly remembered his manners. "Oh, I almost forgot. John Salton, also known as Free Throw, this is my stepdad, Gordon Thoreau."

"It's a pleasure, Mr. Thoreau," Free Throw said politely.

"*Gordon* will do nicely," Matt's stepdad said as he shook Free Throw's hand. "Shall we go? Matt made me put extra money in the meter in case your plane was late, but I think our time is about up." He motioned toward the doors.

After Free Throw was lifted into the van, Matt climbed in and sat beside him. It seemed strange talking to Free Throw in the flesh after all these months of just computer chat.

★ ★ ★

When they arrived home, the rest of the family came barrelling out of the house to greet Matt's friend. Together, the Eagletail-Thoreaus made quite a sight.

"Hello everyone. I've heard a lot about all of you," Free Throw said once he was back sitting in his chair and facing the crowd of people who were Matt's family.

"I'm Colleen," Matt's mom smiled and extended her hand, "and I'm very glad you're finally here. Matt's been so looking forward to your visit."

"Pleased to meet you, ma'am," Free Throw said, smiling and shaking her extended hand. "And you must be Jazz," he said, wheeling over to the tall blond girl. "Matt tells me you're a Raptors fan."

Jazz grinned self-consciously. "You bet. Are you a fan too?" she asked, motioning to his jacket.

Free Throw shook his head. "I've got to stick with the Lakers. Actually, this is for you," he handed her the coat. "When I heard what a great —"

"Hmmph," Matt cleared his throat.

Free Throw nodded. "What a great *fan* of the game you are, I thought I'd bring you this jacket I got at the last Raptors game I went to."

Jazz's eyes grew wide as she accepted the gift. "Wow,

thanks! You've seen them play live? Man, what a treat. All we get is televised games, and not many of them," she sighed.

"We can talk more later, if you'd like," Free Throw smiled warmly at her. "It's not often I get to talk to a girl who plays."

The rest of the family continued with the introductions until Free Throw was thoroughly confused. Two sets of identical twins have that effect on people.

"And we've heard tons about you, too," Marigold said eagerly. "Do you have to sit still all day in your wheelchair?" she asked in the next breath.

Matt flinched, but Free Throw smiled at her. "Sure do. Which one are you, Marigold or Daisy?" he asked.

"I'm Marigold. You can tell it's me and not Daisy because I'm older, by two and a half minutes," she explained as she jerked a small thumb at her chest and beamed proudly.

Free Throw nodded. "I can see that now, Marigold. Would you like to come closer and see how this thing works?" He patted the arm on his wheelchair.

"Me too!" chimed in Daisy as she rushed forward and began to run her fingers over one of the wheels.

Matt realized he'd have to stop acting like he was walking on eggshells around Free Throw. Of course the younger kids would be curious about the wheelchair. He simply wasn't used to having a friend who had his own set of wheels. Matt waited as Free Throw showed the younger girls all the pertinent parts of his chair and answered about a zillion questions.

"Do your hands get dirty?" Violet asked, watching her little sister wiping the dust off her hands and onto her clean jeans.

"Actually, I don't handle the wheel itself, just this metal ring which doesn't touch the ground. In fact, I hardly get dirty at all." He showed Violet how he moved the chair.

"And do you have to put air in the tires like a car?" Rosemary asked.

Free Throw nodded. "Sure do. About sixty-five psi, which is more than a car. I also have my own seatbelt to keep me from slipping out of the chair." He showed the girls the ends of the seatbelt.

"Does your butt get tired sitting all day?" Daisy asked.

"Daisy, don't be rude," Matt's mom interjected.

"It's okay, Mrs. Eagletail-Thoreau. As a matter of fact, Daisy, sometimes I do get a little numb in the bum, but they build these things with pretty comfortable seats, so it's not so bad." Free Throw finished explaining every little detail about his being in a wheelchair until all the girls were satisfied it really wasn't such a strange contraption after all.

Violet and Rosemary were even more interested in Free Throw than the younger girls. In fact, after a while, they almost took over the conversation with each one trying to outdo the other in the odd question department.

"I think that's enough for now, girls. How about we all go into the house for some refreshments?" Matt's mom asked. "Free Throw's come a long way and he could probably use a drink of lemonade and a bite to eat."

"Oh boy! Cake!" the youngest twins added enthusiastically.

As the family moved toward the house, Matt could tell his friend was a hit. He noticed Violet and Rosemary stayed with Free Throw as they went inside, continuing their interrogation on the way. Well, Free Throw had said he wanted to get to know a typical Canadian family. Nothing like getting thrown in the deep end, Matt thought, following the crowd as they went indoors.

★ ★ ★

The next couple of hours were spent getting settled in. Matt found out Free Throw was incredibly strong for a kid his age. He could get in and out of his wheelchair just using his arms. It was impressive.

When the boys were finally alone in Matt's freshly cleaned room, Matt could wait no longer. It was time to discuss the summer ball league.

"Hey Free Throw, you know how you've been saying you'd like to get into coaching?" he began.

Free Throw, who was busy stuffing T-shirts into a

drawer, looked over at Matt and nodded. "Yeah, one day, maybe." He continued stuffing.

"What if I had a way for you to begin your illustrious coaching career now?" Matt rushed on. He felt oddly embarrassed, as if he was making Free Throw do something he didn't want to do. "You see, there's this ball league, the Rocky Mountain Summer Basketball League, and if we can get a team together we would have a chance to try new stuff out and keep up our skills through the summer. It could be a lot of fun." His voice trailed off. "If you're interested, that is. We don't have to if you'd rather not." He looked at his friend and waited.

Matt felt awkward. Maybe Free Throw had only been telling him all that stuff about wanting to coach basketball so they'd have something in common. Maybe he had no intentions of pursuing a career in sports because of, of . . . everything.

Free Throw pushed the overfull drawer closed and looked at Matt with an expression that was impossible to read. He looked like he was deciding on something. Matt swallowed.

Free Throw began slowly nodding his head, then his face split into a wide grin. "A chance to mould some upstart Kobe wannabes into a force on the court; to be able to ream a bunch of jock-heads out and they have to take it; to be able to try out about a thousand new plays I have rattling around in my head? Gee, that's a tough one, Point Guard. When do we start?"

"Whew!" Matt exhaled loudly. "This is great! To tell you the truth, I wasn't sure if you'd want to join up. You'd told me before you hadn't played ball since your accident. I'm really glad you want to join the league. Here's what I've been thinking . . ." Matt told Free Throw all his ideas including which players, how they were going to go about forming a team, and enrolling.

"It sounds good to me," Free Throw agreed. "There's just one thing. If these guys are as good as you say, we'd better sign them up quickly before some other team grabs them."

Matt went into the family room and retrieved the phone book. He got out pencils and paper and together the boys put together their list. Then they began calling.

Matt called his teammates from the Bandits first. Much to his disappointment, he was only able to get Cory Cook, the centre, Larry Chang, a shooting guard, and Ron Klassen, the small forward. The other guys had commitments they couldn't get out of, like a stint at summer camp. Boy, did they howl when they heard they could have been playing basketball instead of doing arts and crafts!

"Even with you as point guard, that still leaves us a lot of men short. Any ideas?" Free Throw said as he examined the roster.

Matt thought for a moment. "As a matter of fact . . ." He began dialling again. Before long, the new team had another small forward, Jimmy Big Bear, and Tony Manyponies, a power forward from Matt's old team, the Tsuu T'ina Warriors. His old teammates thought playing basketball was better than anything else in the world. That was one reason Matt liked them so much. They were serious ball players.

"This is more like it," Free Throw grinned. "We've got a few holes to fill before we're league-ready, but if these guys are as good as you say, I think we have the beginnings of a killer squad." He made a few notes in the margin of his paper. "Are these guys good enough to play other positions if they need to?"

"These guys are the best," Matt said nodding his head. "And tomorrow morning, you're going to see for yourself when they come over for a practice."

★ ★ ★

The next morning, Matt and Free Throw were awakened by a gaggle of geese laughing and yelling in the family room. The girls were watching a cartoon on TV that was evidently hilarious. Matt rolled over and tried to hide his head under his pillow for five more minutes of sleep.

"Come on, Point Guard. We have a practice this morning and I, for one, don't want to be late to meet my new team." Free Throw tossed his pillow at Matt, who groaned.

To get into the main level of the house where the kitchen and dining area was, Matt's stepdad had built a ramp so Free Throw could bypass the stairs and wheel himself up to the veranda, which led to the front door. The covered veranda wrapped around nearly the entire house and offered a spectacular view of the surrounding Alberta countryside.

"Man, you really live in God's country," Free Throw said as he looked out toward the towering mountains to the west. "You are one lucky guy."

Matt nodded. "Yeah, I guess. But what about you down there in sunny San Francisco? You have the ocean practically in your backyard. That's got to be pretty wild."

Free Throw thought a moment. "You know, you're absolutely right. I guess I'm a lucky guy too!"

The two boys headed into the house for a big breakfast of pancakes, bacon, and eggs.

They finished and went back outside as the other members of their new team began arriving. Matt made the introductions.

"John Salton, also known as Free Throw, this is Cory Cook, the captain of the Bandits and centre for our new team." Cory nodded as Matt went on to the next player. "And this is Ron Klassen, small forward; next to him is Larry Chang, our shooting guard."

Both boys bobbed their heads in greeting.

"And these two troublemakers," Matt nodded toward the two bigger players who had come from the

Tsuu T'ina reserve, "are Jimmy Big Bear, small forward, and Tony Manyponies, power forward." The two players nodded at Free Throw.

"You guys are going to make an awesome team," Free Throw said, looking around at the group and whistling through his teeth.

"We think it's great we have our own personal coach." Jimmy smiled at Free Throw. "Matt tells us you really know your stuff."

Free Throw shrugged his shoulders modestly. "You'll be the judge of that." He pulled out his paper and pencil. "Now, down to business. I think our team should have a catchy name so they have something memorable to put on the first place trophy. Any suggestions?"

The guys all thought a moment and several ideas were discussed and rejected.

"How about the Cool Cats?" Ron suggested. "I've always liked animal names."

"Or maybe something really fierce, like the Wildmen," Tony added.

Free Throw nodded, making notes on his paper. "I've got an idea. How about the Wildcats? That way the name is fierce *and* it's an animal. So it's got a little of both, like our team has both First Nations guys and white guys."

Everyone agreed that was a stroke of genius and the Wildcats were born.

"Hey, if we combine our uniforms, we can have

wicked team colours," Larry Chang added. "We could have the purple T-shirts from the Bandits and the white and green shorts from the Warriors. It will look really sharp on the court." This idea was greeted with cheers from the now-excited new team.

The bright sunshine was warm and the smell of summer was in the air as they headed down to the schoolyard where they could have a game.

"Can you make it okay in your chair?" Matt asked. "The forest path isn't the smoothest."

"No problem, Point Guard. This old horse is pretty good with curbs in the city," he patted the arm on his wheelchair." As long as I don't have to jump a yard-high log, I'll be fine."

Matt noticed, however, that Free Throw did up the seatbelt of his chair before they started out. When they reached the schoolyard and its basketball court, the team played until everyone had a feel for each other's moves. As Free Throw and Matt watched, they could see the team really needed more players if it was going to be able to run for a whole game. They needed some *sixth men.*

"Hey, guys. How does the team look?"

Free Throw and Matt turned as Jazz, smiling, walked up to them. Behind her was a slim, dark-haired girl — Mary Blake, Jazz's best friend, and two guys Matt did not know. One appeared to be Matt's age, thirteen, and looked like he'd played basketball all his life. The other boy, who seemed slightly older, must have avoided sports at all costs from the spaghetti-thinness of his arms and legs. Mary played with Jazz on her team at school. Matt remembered that the small, athletic girl had really fast hands and great coordination.

"Guys, this is Mary Blake and her older brothers, Noah and Nigel. They want to join the team too." Jazz indicated the teenage boys who stood beside Mary.

"The Wildcats can always use more players." Matt nodded at Noah and Nigel. He looked at the two brothers. Something was vaguely familiar about both of them. Then Matt realized who Nigel Blake was. He played ball for a team in Calgary that regularly had scouts from the college teams come to check out the older high school players. If he played for them, he must be good. Exactly what the doctor ordered, Matt thought. What a stroke of luck!

"Nigel, it's going to be great having you on our team. We can really use a player of your calibre. Do you mind telling me why you want to join the Wildcats?" Matt asked in a friendly voice, trying not to sound too curious.

"I was going to take the summer off, but changed my mind. I hate being away from the game." The athletic boy shrugged his muscular shoulders. "By the time I tried to find a team in Calgary, everyone already had their rosters full."

"What positions do you like to play?" Matt asked.

Nigel looked him straight in the eye before

answering. "I play only one position — point guard."

"Really?" Matt said lamely. Nigel's tone was cold, but Matt tried to overlook the boy's curt answer. "Well, we can always use another point guard."

Nigel had the same auburn-coloured hair as his sister, but his eyes were brown, not blue, and he was much taller. He moved with an athlete's confidence but had an added touch of arrogance.

Noah, his older brother, was a whole other story. He had mousy brown hair that hung limply in his eyes and thick, black-rimmed glasses that kept sliding down his thin nose. He looked about fourteen, but didn't really have a physique yet. He was more like a cartoon stick drawing of a teenager. Then Matt remembered where he'd seen Noah before. He was the president of the astronomy club at Bragg Creek School and the unfortunate part was, he *looked* like the president of the astronomy club. Well, two out of three kids from one family who played great ball wasn't a bad average.

"We can really use you guys." He nodded, but wondered where they'd be able to play Noah, other than on the bench.

"I don't think you understand, Hotshot," Jazz cut in on Matt's thoughts. "*We* want to join the team, *Mary and I*, as well as the guys."

Matt looked at her and recognized the set of her jaw. She was the most stubborn girl he knew, but this was his team and he called the shots. "The Wildcats are a *guys* team,

Jazz. Noah and Nigel can play, but not you two girls."

Jazz took a step forward. "We'd be an asset to the team and you know it! Quit thinking like a jock. Try to crawl into the twenty-first century and give us a try-out. If we make the cut, great, you have two great ball players. If we bomb, we'll leave, no arguments. What do you say?"

Matt looked from his sister to Free Throw. He knew she had a point. She played better than most boys and Mary was a little dynamo on the court. But this was a guy's team.

He'd noticed the other Wildcats were staying right out of this. Some of them had dealt with Jazz before.

Even Cory Cook, who was practically Jazz's boy-friend, could only shrug his shoulders.

Matt could see he'd get no help from his teammates. He turned to Free Throw. "You're the coach. What do you say?"

Free Throw rested his elbows on the arms of his wheelchair and laced his hands together. "We're an en-lightened people down below the forty-ninth parallel. What if we do what Jazz suggests and give the new Wildcat wannabes an official tryout?"

Matt looked around at the other players on the team. They still weren't saying anything. If he wanted to be fair, he had no choice. Besides, Jazz and Mary against the razor-edged 'Cats? What was he worrying about?

"Grab a ball, Jazz. Ron, you play for the ladies. First

team to six points wins. Free Throw can evaluate every-one's playing." Matt walked out onto the court.

"Sounds fair enough," Jazz agreed, smiling at the other players on her team.

Matt nodded at a large player sitting on the side-lines. "Jimmy, you and the guys are with me." These guys were good. Jazz's team was going down. The two teams formed up at the jump circle.

Cory went against Jazz for the tipoff. It was close, but Cory managed to tap it over to Larry Chang, who turned and started toward the basket. Nigel swooped in and snagged the ball away from Larry. He turned back toward Matt's basket and sailed in for a picture-perfect layup.

Jazz whooped and jumped. "That's two points for the good guys," she crowed.

Matt loped over and retrieved the ball. He inbound-ed it to Cory, who started toward the far net. Jazz and Mary moved to cover him. Matt noticed how grace-fully Mary moved. She was small, but very agile. She had Cory covered in the wink of an eye as Jazz moved in to pressure him, hoping for a turnover.

"Cory!" Matt called. Cory nodded and lobbed a high, long pass.

Noah was covering Matt, but when the ball started arcing down toward Matt, Noah ducked; Matt grabbed the ball and began dribbling. He'd passed the three-point line when Ron smoked up behind him with Jazz hot on his heels. Matt went up and launched.

Swish! Two points. "Okay, Wildcats!" he called, grinning at his sister who stuck out her tongue.

Noah tried to toss the ball in to Mary. He had surprising strength for someone with noodle arms, Matt thought, as he watched the ball sail over Mary's head. Nigel scooped the ball from under Ron's nose and started downcourt. He could ball-handle like a pro. In seconds, the guy was in the paint and the ball was in the net.

"That's four points, Hotshot. One more basket and we're in!" Jazz yelled.

The ball was being worked down the court toward Jazz's net, when Larry tried a pass to Cory, but Nigel picked it off. Three of Matt's team closed on him.

"Nigel, I'm in the clear!" Jazz called.

Nigel ignored her and, instead, tried to weave his way through the defence. Jimmy Big Bear took two steps and powered the ball away from Nigel. Turning, he streaked down to the paint and went in for another two points.

Noah tossed the ball in, but it was too far to Jazz's left for her to grab it as it flew past. Cory ran for it and began a drive.

"Come on, defence, move!" Nigel called. "Ron, watch the weak side. Close it up, Noah, you jerk!" he yelled at his older brother, who didn't seem to know what to do.

Matt saw Mary move over to cover the hole Noah was leaving open. Jazz moved up to partially cover the weak spot left by Mary. They were already playing as a team, Matt thought, as he watched the way the players moved on the court. Cory was nearly to the top of the key before he was stopped. Nigel was awesome. You couldn't get past him. Cory tried to pass to Larry, but Mary shot out and stole the ball.

"Come on, Noah, help me," she called to her brother and together they started toward the net. When they reached the paint, Mary passed Noah the ball. "Just like we practised, Noah, go for it!"

Noah went in for what looked like the world's most awkward layup. It hit the backboard and bounced out. Mary grabbed the rebound and went up. Nothing but net!

"That's six points, Hotshot!" Jazz yelled. "This is sweet." She was so excited she practically danced up to Free Throw.

"What do you say, Coach. Pretty cool, huh?" She flashed a wide victory grin.

"What can I say? You're in! Welcome to the Wildcats!" Free Throw smiled back and shook his head. "This is going to be quite the team!"

"I eagerly anticipate vanquishing our first opponent," Noah said, pushing his glasses back up to the bridge of his nose.

Matt looked at him. "What was that?"

"He says he's looking forward to our first game," Mary interpreted. "He always talks like he swallowed a dictionary. I'm trying to get him to use ordinary words so the rest of the world can understand him, but it's an ongoing battle."

Nigel ignored his brother as though he was a big embarrassment.

As the team walked back to the house, Matt and Free Throw hung back.

"What do you think?" Matt asked his friend.

"I think the Wildcats are going to be great. There's one thing I noticed." Free Throw forced the wheel on his chair over a piece of log. "Nigel is obviously used to being the boss. He might not like taking orders from you. Also, we may have to remind everyone this is a team sport, no one player rules the court."

Matt thought about this. He'd noticed the same things.

"I think once we have a couple of games under our belts, Nigel will straighten out," Free Throw concluded.

Matt hoped he was right. The first rule of team sport was that everyone on the team was equally important. Each player formed part of the chain that made the team strong. If even one player didn't co-operate, he became a weak link, a link that could break the rest of the chain.

3 NO GOOD DEED GOES UNPUNISHED

Matt found out there were a lot of teams signed up for the league.

"I know some of these guys," he said to Free Throw as they went over the roster that had the teams and their players. Matt's eye fell on one name in particular. John Beal. He shook his head. "I thought this creep would be benched for life by now. He's nothing but bad news."

Free Throw read the name. "I take it you know the guy?"

"You might say I've run into him a couple of times." Matt flopped on the family room couch. "You see, when I played for the Tsuu T'ina Warriors, we had a game against the Bragg Creek Bandits when Beal played for them." Here Matt could only shake his head. "That guy played the dirtiest, nastiest basketball known to man. He was forever taking cheap shots, and some got so bad, players were seriously hurt. He's got a *win at all costs* kind of attitude, no matter who gets slam dunked in the process."

Matt put his feet up on the old coffee table. "Beal used to live here in Bragg Creek, but he moved to Calgary when his folks split up. I think he lived with his aunt and he got into a lot of trouble. I always thought I'd see his name in the headlines in some big showdown with the police. He was on a one-way trip to trouble and the really strange part was that Beal seemed to like it."

Matt put his hands behind his head. "There was one game I'll never forget. We were one point apart and the clock was ticking. I got a fast break and smoked downcourt. I was going in for one of my no-fail layups, when out of the blue, Beal blindsides me. Not a gentle tap either; I'm talking knock-me-down, winded, serious pain. Then Beal bends over me and I thought he was checking to see if I was okay. No way. He tells me to stay out of his way or there would be more of the same and next time, I wouldn't walk away."

Matt shrugged his shoulders. "You had to know I wasn't going to take that lying down, despite the fact I was flat on my back on the floor. I got up and covered Beal so closely, I could have been his shadow. I was in his face every second that remained of the game. He got so mad I thought his eyes were going to pop out of his head. He was cursing me and trying all sorts of dirt, but I kept on playing," Matt grinned. "Without him stomping all over the Warrior ball-handlers, we almost, but not quite, pulled off a win. Man, we were so close I thought we had it. After I spoiled every remaining chance he had to score, Beal vowed he'd get me. Fortunately, I never played against him again."

"Man, that's quite the story! What are you going to do when the Wildcats go up against his team?" Free Throw asked, genuinely interested.

Matt thought a moment. "Watch my back. I bleed too easily to take him on without help. Besides, maybe I'm worrying for nothing. Maybe he's changed. One thing's for sure: I'd really like to beat him, just once, to even things up. I don't like being anyone's doormat, and that's how he made me feel."

★ ★ ★

The next afternoon, Rosemary and Violet were in the family room arguing noisily about who would get to sit next to Free Throw at supper when Matt walked in on them.

"Why don't you two take Precious for a walk? It's a nice day and you should all get out of the house." He looked over at the big dog snoring peacefully on the carpet. "See, he really wants to go for a walk, don't you, Precious?"

Contentedly, the dog snorted in his sleep. "That means *yes* in dog talk," Matt assured the twins, who were eyeing him skeptically. When neither girl made any move, he sighed. "Come on, you two, Free Throw needs a break from his munchkin fan club. We have to discuss basketball strategy."

"I told you to leave him alone!" Marigold admonished her sister.

"Me! You're the one that wanted to have a ride in his wheelchair — like that big butt of yours could fit into a chair that size!" Rosemary sniffed indignantly.

Matt thought this was silly, as he was pretty sure both of their skinny eight-year-old butts could easily have fit into the chair at the same time. The girls left the room arguing over which of them Free Throw liked best. Matt shook his head.

He and Free Throw were going to meet the team at the schoolyard for an official practice on the outdoor court. Their first league game was tomorrow. As they made their way down the path that led to the school-yard, Matt heard yelling behind him.

"Can we come?" two voices chimed together.

"Oh man!" Matt cursed under his breath. "I'll tell them not today," he said to Free Throw as Rosemary and Violet caught up with them.

"No worries, Matt. I don't have any little sisters and I really do enjoy their company." Free Throw winked at the two girls as they each grabbed onto the back of his chair. "Let's go, ladies." He began wheeling the chair down the path again as Matt followed, frowning.

Free Throw's strong arms propelled his wheel-chair along the forest path like it was rolling on fresh pavement instead of a maze of criss-crossed tree roots, large stones, and washouts. The small girls kept up a running commentary of stories about what berries and flowers they liked best and how Matt said squirrels were just gophers with good PR and did Free Throw think there were any bears on this particular path? Their high, childish voices mingled with the chattering of the birds until Matt could hardly tell where the girls left off and the birds began.

When they reached the outdoor basketball court at the school, the girls left to play on the swings while Matt began dribbling the ball and warming up. Free Throw sat on the side, reading his playbook.

"Hey, Free Throw, can I ask you something I've been wondering about?" Matt asked, as he did a perfect fadeaway jumper.

"Shoot," his friend said, not looking up as he scribbled notes in the margin of the book.

"Why don't you have one of those fancy electric wheelchairs I see people at the mall using?" He tried an unsuccessful sky-hook from an outrageous distance.

Free Throw stopped writing and looked so serious Matt thought he'd offended his friend.

"Hey, man, you don't have to explain to me. I was curious, that's all." Matt looked at his friend's face. Free Throw's eyes clouded, then he sighed.

"I'm going to tell you something I've never told anyone." He shifted in his chair. "After I got out of the hospital, I kept telling myself the doctors were wrong. They didn't know squat about my body. I was an athlete, used to training hard. All I had to do to walk again was train a little harder."

Matt had stopped dribbling the ball and was listening closely now.

Free Throw avoided his gaze as he went on. "My folks wanted to buy me an electric chair, but I told them I didn't want one. What I didn't tell them was I thought I was going to walk again, so I wouldn't need an expensive electric number when the manual one I had would do me for the time I needed any chair."

He sighed and tossed his pen down on his book. "Then, after a while, I discovered training wasn't going to cut it. I wasn't going to walk again and I had better accept it. But I'd become used to this old chair and using it kept my upper body strong so I could do more things for myself." He shrugged his shoulders. "Dumb, huh?"

Matt swallowed. He'd never met anyone who was as brave as this guy was. "All that means is you aren't a quitter. You never gave up until you'd done everything you could to fix the problem. I think it shows you're a pretty tough dude." The two boys exchanged a look that said more than words.

Just then, Matt spotted Jazz and Mary coming across the field toward them. Unconsciously, Matt straightened up as he watched Mary approaching.

"Where are the rest of the guys?" Jazz asked as she strode up.

"They'll be here soon, Miss Jasmine." Free Throw said in a gentlemanly voice, then nodded at Mary. "Hey."

"Oh, hi Free Throw," Mary looked around, then continued toward Matt.

Her face broke into a bright smile as she walked up to him. "Want to try a little one-on-one?" she asked. Winking, she grabbed the ball away from Matt, who was so surprised he made no attempt to stop her. She pivoted and dribbled out of his reach.

Matt stood perfectly still, watching her. He'd never noticed how blue her eyes were before. "You're on, Blake."

At that moment, a loud wailing from the direction of the stream that ran past the far edge of the playground made everyone turn.

"That sounds like Rosemary!" Jazz started running in the direction of the sound.

It was then Matt noticed neither girl was in sight. He was sure they had both been here a minute ago, bothering him and Free Throw. He swallowed and started running after Jazz, his heart pounding as the wailing turned into a scream.

Within seconds, they were at the stream and could immediately see the problem. Rosemary had climbed a tree overhanging the creek and, unfortunately, the branch she'd been on had not been able to hold her weight and had cracked almost in two. Maybe she'd been wrong about which twin had the bigger butt, Matt thought, assessing the situation. She was now dangling by her hands from the broken branch as the small mountain stream rushed below her.

Matt wouldn't have been so worried, except somehow, Rosemary had managed to climb to quite a height. It would be a long fall before his screaming stepsister hit the water. It would serve her right to get a thorough dunking, he grumbled as he tried to figure out the easiest way to get her down.

"I'm coming, Rosemary! Stop thrashing around, you're going to break the branch completely off." He moved under the ancient tree and looked up. It was a very tall tree. He was too short to reach even the first branch.

"Rosie, how did you get up there?" Matt was acutely aware of Mary watching him. It made his face feel hot, but he liked the idea of Mary seeing him do such a good deed.

Rosemary stopped wiggling while she answered. "Violet stood on my shoulders and grabbed onto that first branch, then she leaned over and helped me shinny up." She hiccupped back a sob. "But then dopey Violet jumped down and went home without me, so I decided to explore the tree by myself. Matty, my arms are falling off, I can't hold on much longer," the frightened eight-year-old wailed.

"Free Throw, can you move over under the tree so I can stand on your chair to get to that low hanging branch?" Matt asked.

His friend nodded and quickly wheeled over. "I've got a great idea, Point Guard. Climb onto the arm rests, and then I'll give you a leg up."

Matt climbed onto the wheelchair, balancing on the small arm rests. Gingerly, he put his foot into Free Throw's locked hands. With an incredible feat of strength, Free Throw hoisted Matt up high enough for him to grab the branch and swing himself up into the tree. Scrambling up the rough bark of the old poplar, Matt picked his way through the leafy branches to Rosemary.

"Take my hand," Matt said, not daring to move too far out onto the branch for fear of breaking it off completely.

"I'm afraid to let go. I'll fall into the river," she sobbed.

"Rosie, it's not a river. It's barely big enough to be called a creek. I've had baths that were deeper than it is, for crying out loud. Now grab on, I won't let you fall." Holding onto a nearby branch to steady himself, Matt reached out for her. As he did, he could hear the cracked limb he was standing on groan under the extra weight.

Then everything happened really fast.

With a shudder, the branch splintered and snapped.

Rosemary screamed and reached for Matt, who caught her hand before the entire end of the broken limb fell into the bubbling water below. Out of options, Matt wrapped his legs around the remaining stump, as he held onto his terrified sister with one hand.

"Free Throw, can you move closer to the edge of the bank and I'll drop her down to you?" Matt yelled, as he tightened his grip on his sister. She was now clinging to him with both of her small hands and sobbing loudly. His own arm felt like it was coming out of its socket, but they were now hanging over the rocky bank of the stream and Rosemary's landing would be worse there than if Matt had let her drop into the stream, where the water would have broken her fall.

"Gotcha, Point Guard," Free Throw said, manoeuvring into position beneath the struggling girl.

Matt held his breath, then opened his hand. Rosemary shrieked as she dropped through the air and landed on Free Throw with a thud. He caught her easily and she came to rest safely in his lap.

"I wish my stupid sister was here to see me now," Rosemary whimpered, wiping the tears from her dirty face.

Matt sighed with relief, and then noticed Mary still watching him. He couldn't resist a little showing off. He grinned and waved.

"Nothing to it!" he said, swinging himself back up onto the branch so he could climb down. He'd almost made it when he stepped on a green twig that bent beneath his weight. With a panicked yell, he felt himself tumble off the branch and into empty air.

4 RIDING THE PINE

Matt hit the ground with a thump. The wind was knocked out of him and he knew from the odd tingling sensation that his legs hadn't done so well. He'd protected his head, but his legs had been twisted around and stretched backward.

"Oh my God!" Jazz cried, rushing forward. "Did he hit you?" she asked Free Throw anxiously.

"I'm fine, really," Free Throw reassured her. "But maybe we'd better check on Matt." He moved over to his fallen friend.

Matt lay flat on the ground, unable to move. He still couldn't take a breath and talking was out of the question. He tried, but only succeeded in gasping noiselessly like a fish out of water.

"He doesn't look so good," Jazz observed, poking her stepbrother with the toe of her shoe. "Maybe we'd better get some help." She frowned as she stood looking down at Matt, who lay staring up at them, still unable to speak.

"I think that's a good idea," Mary agreed nervously as both girls sprinted back to the house.

Rosemary wiggled off her perch on Free Throw's lap. She looked at her stepbrother's stricken form and blanched. "I have to go now, I think I hear my mom calling." She dashed after Jazz and Mary.

Free Throw calmly waited beside his friend. With his fingers laced and slumping down in his chair, he reminded Matt of a statue of Buddha. Suddenly, Matt coughed, then pulled a long, ragged breath into his burning lungs.

"You okay, buddy?" Free Throw asked calmly, but there was concern and a trace of fear, in his voice. "It's really nasty to get winded like that."

"I think so," Matt rasped, "But my legs hurt. It feels like I twisted my ankles starting at my thighs." He lay on the ground for a moment, sucking in deep breaths, and stared up at the tree he'd so recently been showing off in. After a couple of minutes, his chest stopped hurting and he could breathe almost normally.

"Well, all in all, I'd say that was pretty stupid," Matt winced, then started to laugh. "Ow, that hurts!" he groaned and grabbed his stomach, laughing even harder. "Ow, ow, ow!"

Free Throw took one look at him writhing on the ground and couldn't help himself. Matt looked so pathetic, Free Throw had to start chuckling too. "Stop moving around in case you've broken something."

"Oh, I broke something all right," Matt said, tears of laughter streaming down his face, "the sound barrier as I crashed to the ground!"

"You know what your biggest problem is, Point Guard?" Free Throw said between bouts of laughter.

"What?" Matt asked, trying to control himself.

"From where I sit, I'd say your landing!" Both boys cracked up again as they waited for help to come.

It wasn't long before they heard a van pulling up. Matt looked over at the pretty, dark-haired woman who climbed out of the vehicle and walked quickly toward them.

"*Bonjour*, Matt," said Dr. Judith Samson, the mobile veterinarian, in a thick French-Canadian accent. "The girls couldn't get hold of your parents, and the only doctor they could think of was me. So, voila, I am here." With a confident smile, she bent to examine Matt.

Free Throw turned his chair around and wheeled away.

After a brief exam, Dr. Samson shook her head. "I think you have no broken bones, only severely distended tendons." She gave him a wry look. "If you were a dog, I would recommend complete crate rest for a week with an anti-inflammatory medication to control the swelling. But for you, I think we should go see a human doctor right now. I will take you."

"A human doctor?" Matt asked, grinning, but he knew what the pretty young vet meant. She'd treated

Precious on more than one occasion and had always been one hundred percent correct in her diagnoses. The vet managed to get Matt into the back of the van, but before he would allow her to take him to the doctor, he called Free Throw over. Matt could see his friend's face was grey.

"My legs are fine, Free Throw. A little bruised and banged up. Will you go back to the house and tell the girls what's happening?"

Free Throw took a deep breath, and then exhaled loudly. He nodded solemnly at Matt. "Are you sure your legs are okay?"

Dr. Samson could see the concern on the young man's face. She put her hand on Free Throw's shoulder. "He will be okay. I haven't been wrong in a diagnosis in a long time, and I don't plan on starting with this two-legged animal."

Turning, she smiled reassuringly at Matt. "I can hardly wait to hear the story of how this happened. I always thought you were the sensible one." She closed the van door and waved at Free Throw. Through the side window, Matt watched his friend's worried face as they drove away.

★ ★ ★

Matt tried for the third time to make it up the ramp to the veranda in the wheelchair the doctor had loaned him until his legs healed. It had been exactly as Dr. Samson had said. He'd severely strained the muscles in his legs and had to rest them for about a week. And it was going to be an extremely long week if he didn't get the hang of this crazy chair.

"Try pushing on the wheels like this." Free Throw showed him how to manoeuvre up the gently sloping ramp. "It takes a little practice, but you can do it."

Matt tried again and this time, he made it. "Great! I thought I was going to have to live with take-out delivered to the family room." With some effort, Matt made it to the kitchen table. The rest of the family was waiting. Rosemary had refused to talk to Matt since the accident. She'd blamed herself and wouldn't listen when Matt had said he'd fallen because he wasn't being careful. He didn't mention the fact he was showing off at the time.

"What about the game tomorrow?" Jazz asked as they started eating, letting Matt know where his health stood on her list of priorities. "You're leaving us pretty short-handed."

"I think we'll have enough players. You guys won't be off the court a lot, though." Matt shook his head, anger at himself boiling up. "I feel so crappy about this. It was a stupid accident that could have been avoided."

Rosemary looked down at her plate. Matt noticed his stepsister's quivering lip and sighed, regretting his outburst.

"Rosie, for the hundredth time, it wasn't your fault." He rolled his eyes.

"I thought the rescue part was pretty spectacular," Free Throw added, trying to make the little girl feel better. "I had no idea you were that athletic, Rosemary. Have you ever thought about a career in the circus as a trapeze artist?"

Rosemary thought about this for a moment. "I did do a fabulous landing *in your lap*," she smiled demurely at Free Throw, then gave Violet a toothy grin. Violet had been feeling sorely left out ever since she'd heard about the daredevil rescue and the dramatic three-point landing. Apparently satisfied everything was right in the universe again and that she was ahead of her sister in Free Throw points, Rosemary brightened, then hungrily began eating.

"Can we get back to the game tomorrow?" Jazz said, exasperated at the turn the conversation had taken. "And speaking of basketball," she paused a fraction of a second. "I heard Beal's team is burning up the courts."

Matt tried to be casual. "Yeah, I think I heard the same thing. No worries, Jazz. The 'Cats can handle Beal." He looked over at her. "*I* can handle Beal."

"I think I have a couple of sweet plays which should give the Wildcats their first win," Free Throw said confidently, smoothly changing the subject.

"I'm glad you're so sure, because we're playing the Springbank Spurs and I know some of the guys on that team. They're good." Jazz shook her head.

Matt shrugged nonchalantly. "So are we."

★ ★ ★

"What happened to you?" Jimmy Big Bear asked, staring in disbelief as Matt and Free Throw both wheeled into the dressing room at the Springbank Community Centre where the Wildcats would play the Spurs. The rest of the guys stopped and stared.

"It appears you've been beset by an unfortunate circumstance," Noah observed.

Matt flinched. He'd been dreading telling his teammates he couldn't play. "Yeah, you could sort of say that. Actually, I had a little problem rescuing my kid stepsister from a tree," Matt said, trying to explain the incident away as quickly as possible. He hoped they could move on to the emergency plays Free Throw had come up with to compensate for the man short.

"Jeez, Matt, you look pretty torn up." Cory said sympathetically.

"Don't worry. It would take more than a little face-plant to keep the Cloud Leaper down," Tony added as he gave Matt a friendly punch on the arm.

At the mention of his nickname, Matt felt better. He'd received it because when it came to out-jumping everyone on the court, his legs were spring-loaded. He could jump higher and move faster than most guys half a metre taller, which was a good thing, because he was always the shortest guy on the team. He relaxed a little in his wheelchair.

"I guess your clumsiness solves the problem of who will be the starting point guard," Nigel said as he grabbed a water bottle out of his gym bag. "Not that it was going to be a problem as far as I was concerned," he added, with a trace of a smirk that Matt couldn't help but notice.

Matt ignored Nigel's snide remark. It wouldn't do any good to start arguing now. "Okay, guys. Free Throw, genius coach that he is, has come up with a few plays that will not only keep us in the game, but are going to win it for us." The other guys gathered around. Nigel, however, hung back as though Free Throw's plays were nothing special.

"We've made some changes, Nigel. You should listen up," Matt suggested.

Nigel glared at him, then moved over to join the rest of the team.

Matt listened to Free Throw as he went over the plays. Mary and Jazz had already been brought up to speed and Matt knew they'd have no problem. When the team hit the floor, Matt was confident the Wildcats were going to win.

As the game progressed, Matt found it extremely difficult to sit on the sidelines and watch. He wanted to get out of that chair and grab the ball, then go in for a layup and put some points on the board for the good guys. Instead, he sat and watched as his buddies raced downcourt with the ball. Sitting there, doing nothing, was one of the hardest things he'd ever done. Glancing over at Free Throw, Matt couldn't help but admire his friend. He was cheering his team on, changing and coming up with plays out of the blue like this was what he'd always planned to do with his life.

The shrill of the whistle brought Matt's attention back to the game. The Spurs had the lead, but the Wildcats were determined to win and, as the clock ran down, had pulled out all the stops. Matt felt guilty. He should be out there, not sitting here like an unlucky mascot.

"Okay, you guys, here's the plan," Free Throw said as the players came off the court for a time out. He quickly explained the play, complete with a diagram using different coloured markers for each team.

"I think I can get past those two jokers the Spurs call guards. The rest of you just need to feed me the ball," Nigel instructed the other players. Matt saw Jimmy's face darken.

"It's whoever's in the best scoring position that will take the ball, Nigel. This team works together. Everyone has special skills which are going to help us win," Matt said firmly.

"Well spoken, Matt. An oration with sage advice," Noah solemnly intoned.

Matt looked at Noah. He hadn't played so far this game, but his enthusiasm was still evident.

Mary shook her head. "Again, Noah."

"What the geek's trying to say is he thinks Matt's right," Nigel interrupted, obviously annoyed. "But the whole purpose of the game is to win and that's what I'm going to do." He shoved past his brother, knocking him out of the way as he walked back out onto the court.

"Nice," Jimmy commented wryly as he followed Nigel.

Jazz shrugged her shoulders. "He needs to take a pill instead of being one."

The team hit the court like they had a secret weapon, which they did — and his name was Free Throw.

"Overhead!" Jimmy called to Cory, the tall Wildcats centre, who was over the half-court line and trying to make his way through traffic. Cory fired the ball to Jimmy. He jumped and snagged it, then started dribbling hard.

"Pass me the ball," Nigel called.

"I've got a clear lane," Jimmy yelled, ignoring Nigel, who was surrounded by Spurs. The Spurs defence wasn't about to let one lone player break through their line. Immediately, two other players left their men and covered Jimmy. Mary and Jazz cut to the weak side.

"Jimmy, pass!" Jazz called in her loudest voice.

"I'm in the clear!" Mary chimed in. "Pass to me!"

Again the Spurs defence responded. This time they

turned for the girls. That's when Jimmy fired a chest pass to Cory, who had sprinted down close to the baseline. He turned and, driving into the paint under the basket, pulled off a perfect reverse layup. The Spurs' lead dropped by two.

With time running out, the Wildcats needed possession of the ball. Jimmy managed to force a pass, which Mary intercepted. She had barely turned toward the Spurs' basket when she was fouled by one of their big guards. The ref blew the whistle.

Mary's free throws were a thing of beauty. Matt smiled as he watched the petite girl at the top of the key. He'd never noticed how effective and versatile a player she was before. Maybe this was a silver lining to his being in this chair. It gave him a whole new perspective on the game, and on one special player.

Swish! The Spurs lead went down again. Matt clapped his hands and whistled. He noticed Mary look over at him and smile as she ran back to her defensive position.

The Wildcats needed one more basket and they'd have their first win. Matt wished the Cloud Leaper were out there helping. They had another substitution: Tony was in, Jazz was out. The clock was ticking down.

The teams took their positions. Cory was focusing on his jump. Matt knew from the way he was standing that he was going to tip the ball to Mary, who'd immediately pass to Tony, who would start downcourt.

They'd practised this fast breakaway ploy and it was a sure winner.

Mary grabbed the tipoff, but when she turned to pass to Tony, one of the Spurs moved with surprising speed to intercept. In a flash, Nigel cut in front, took the pass and, ignoring his other teammates, headed for the basket. Jimmy had made his way to a hole right under the net, but Nigel ignored him as he manoeuvred through traffic. Stopping at the last second, Nigel made a great pump fake and went up for a picture-perfect jumpshot.

Swish! Two winning points! The crowd thundered its approval. They were still yelling and clapping as the final whistle blew and the team jogged off the court. Matt saw his family cheering in the stands and it felt funny not to be on the court and part of the win. He really wanted out of this wheelchair.

The team went wild too. Noah was slapping his other teammates on the back and congratulating them. He'd only played about five minutes, and even then he'd picked up a foul, but he had played and he felt a part of the team.

Jazz punched Matt on the arm. "And you didn't want us on your team!" she laughed.

Matt rubbed his arm. "I didn't want *you*. Mary was okay," he teased, smiling at the petite, brown-haired girl who was still bouncing with excitement.

Mary moved over to him, patting him affectionately

on the head. "Wildcats rule! Matt, you should have been there," she giggled. "I'm just teasing. We couldn't have done it without you sitting here . . . watching . . . Let me put it another way. Thanks for your support." She smiled so warmly at him, he couldn't help but grin foolishly back at her. The team headed for the showers to change before going out for victory burgers.

As Matt and Free Throw waited for the team, Matt went over the game again in his head. "That last play was something. Nigel really pulled it off," he said, looking out across the field to the trees beyond.

"But . . ." Free Throw added. "I can hear a *but* in there."

"Jimmy was in the clear and there was no doubt he could have scored that basket if Nigel had passed to him," Matt said, still looking at the trees.

"Nigel does seem to have a problem playing as part of a team," Free Throw agreed. "But he is effective. He gets results."

"But he makes everyone else feel like an idiot out there and I don't think that's cool," Matt said and began turning his wheelchair toward the ramp, which led to the parking lot.

As he turned, Nigel, who had come up behind them, noisily dropped his bag on the ground. "I can't make it for burgers," he said coldly, zipping up a light windbreaker. Without another word, he picked up his bag and started out to the parking lot and a waiting friend's car. Matt wondered how much of the conversation he'd overheard.

★ ★ ★

"That was quite the win," Matt's stepdad said as they settled down in the family room to watch a video.

"Man, I'll say," Free Throw agreed. "The Wildcats have never been beaten. Very impressive record."

Matt raised an eyebrow. "You do remember this was their first game?" he asked.

"A minor detail, Point Guard. Wait and see. My team's going all the way!" He folded his arms and looked very smug.

"Do you think you two will be up for our trip to the Calgary Stampede tomorrow?" Matt's mom asked as she handed each of the boys a plate with three tacos on it. The family had planned on taking Free Throw to the world-famous event, but that was before Matt had injured himself.

"Count me in," Free Throw said, accepting his plate.

Matt wasn't sure if he could do it. He was, after all, in a wheelchair.

"What's the matter, Point Guard? You worried I won't be able to keep up?" Free Throw took a huge bite of his crunchy taco. "Hey, these are better than the ones we get in the States. You must have a secret ingredient." He nodded at Matt's mom.

"I do, and I'm not telling or it wouldn't be a secret anymore," she said evasively.

Matt looked at his friend. No way would he let him down." No problem!" he said brightly. "In fact, I was wondering what we should do first tomorrow. The midway is always my favourite." He took a bite of his taco. What was he nervous about? He was the same kid who went to the Stampede every year. He just wouldn't be walking this time.

5 BAD GUYS ALWAYS WEAR BLACK HATS

The bright July sun was already hot and it wasn't even noon yet. Matt and his family were at the world-famous Calgary Stampede, where the spirit of the Old West was celebrated by North America's best cowboys competing in rough-and-tough rodeo events and chuck wagon races. The smell of hotdogs and cotton candy was everywhere. They had decided to take in the midway first with its festive carnival atmosphere, and Matt's mom was busily planning their strategy.

"Okay, we'll meet back here at two o'clock to go to the infield events. Remember to keep your money out of sight," Colleen warned. "And don't eat any meat that hasn't been refrigerated and then cooked in front of you," she added. "Oh, and Jazz and Mary, don't talk to any strange boys. These carnie people . . ."

Jazz rolled her eyes and Mary giggled. Jazz had invited her along and Matt had been really glad when he'd found out she was coming.

"Mom!" Matt groaned. "We're not six years old.

68

We'll be okay." He shook his head. "You'd think you have enough babies to look after with those four geese." He nodded at the young twins, who promptly began complaining at the term *babies*.

Jazz smiled. "Shall we go, gentlemen?" she asked Matt and Free Throw. The four of them waved goodbye and headed down the noisy midway.

Mary walked beside Matt. She'd pinned one side of her hair up with one of Jazz's barrettes and Matt decided it looked a lot nicer in Mary's hair than in his stepsister's.

Jazz liked the bumper cars best and wasn't shy about showing the rest of the helpless participants how the ride got its name. Mary thought that bingo was less dangerous and made Jazz sit with them through three games. When they came to the roller coaster and then the Zipper, Matt couldn't help but feel a little left out as he and Free Throw waited while the girls went on the rides. He'd always gone on the wickedest ones and found it frustrating to sit and watch.

"That was too much fun!" Mary bubbled when she and Jazz alighted from the parachute drop.

Matt nodded, looking up at her. "It sure looked like it. Next year I'm putting it on the top of my hit list." He tried to sound enthusiastic, but something in his voice must have given him away.

Mary looked thoughtful. "Hey, I'd really like to play some games — you know, something we can all do.

Come on, it will be the girls against the guys."

"Right on!" Jazz immediately agreed. She was the most competitive person Matt had ever known and she always played for keeps. Maybe that's what made her so deadly on the basketball court.

"Let's go, unless you're afraid you'll get thrashed by a couple of girls." Jazz grinned at Matt. "Come on, Hotshot, or are you chicken?" She began dancing around flapping her arms and crowing.

"Okay, okay," Matt laughed. "And FYI Jazz, roosters crow, chickens go *bock, bock, bock.*" He tried to imitate the sound he thought a respectable hen would make, but stopped when people started staring. Suddenly embarrassed in front of Mary, he cleared his throat. "Come on, Free Throw. We've got work to do." The four of them headed for the games of chance.

They all tried ring toss and Mary came closest to winning, but when it came to one called Whack-a-Mole, Matt did very well, managing to smack the greatest number of mechanical moles as they randomly popped their heads up then retreated. He also tried, unsuccessfully, to win Mary a big stuffed dinosaur at the dart game. Free Throw, however, easily won at the rifle range and gave his prize, a pink teddy bear, to Jazz, telling her it was to keep Fuzzy Bunny, her favourite old stuffed toy, company.

After several more games along the midway the contest ended with everyone agreeing they were all so awesome, it must be a tie. The four decided to stop for corndogs. Jazz and Mary ordered, then it was Matt's turn, but before he could speak, the man asked Jazz if *he* wanted one too, indicating Matt with his thumb.

"Why don't you ask him?" Jazz said indignantly.

The man turned to Matt and said very slowly and loudly, "Do . . . you . . . want . . . one?" He indicated the corndogs.

Matt felt his temper start to rise. He gave the man a look that said he was a jerk, but answered politely, "Yes please, and I suggest you ask my friend if he wants one too."

Free Throw nodded. "Sure, I'll have one too."

When they left the vendor, Matt was still angry. "What a jerk. I can't walk, but I can understand English just fine."

"You'll get used to it," Free Throw said, taking a huge bite of his corndog. "A lot of people get disabilities confused. They think because you're physically challenged, you aren't as smart or you can't take care of yourself. Don't worry about it."

But Matt thought it was really insulting. He'd never come up against these problems before. He remembered taking the commuter train down here. It was supposed to be accessible for people with disabilities, except the platform and the cars didn't line up, so it was really hard to get on and off the train. It was so frustrating when the street curb was a little too high or a building had even one step — all things he'd never thought about before. Being in a wheelchair was a real eye-opener.

After the corndogs, they also had cotton candy and a bag each of tiny donuts for dessert. Matt could have eaten about a dozen bags of those donuts. He was also adjusting to not being able to see past people, or having ticket vendors miss him because he was so much lower in his chair. They decided they were going to go into the exhibition hall to see a photo exhibit Mary had read about, when Matt discovered the only way in was a flight of stairs.

"What kind of a Mickey Mouse place is this?" he asked, frustrated and angry.

"It's okay, Matt. A lot of older buildings aren't wheelchair accessible. We'll go somewhere else while the girls view the exhibit," Free Throw said calmly.

Matt was tired and his legs ached. "That's not good enough. The Stampede has a million visitors a year. How can they not make it easy for everyone to see their stupid exhibits?" He looked up at the stairs, which seemed to go on forever.

"Hey Beautiful, why don't you ditch the wheel-chair wonder and hang with me?"

The voice was unmistakable.

Matt wheeled his chair around and stared into the grinning face of John Beal. He was taller than Matt had remembered and he'd really filled out. He looked about sixteen in his trendy polo shirt and baggy jeans.

He wore a black cowboy hat, which he pushed back on his head exposing his short brown hair.

Beal had a really nasty smirk on his face as he watched for Matt's reaction. "I'm on my way to meet my buddies, but when I saw you, I thought I'd take a detour and say hi." He smiled broadly at Mary.

"I thought you were history, Beal. Thrown out with the rest of the trash." Matt pulled himself up in his chair. Beal could push Matt's buttons just by being in the same universe with him.

"No such luck, Indian boy, no thanks to you. I'm still around to spread a little sunshine in your boring lives. In fact, we've moved back — I'm returning to good old Bragg Creek Junior High next year." His eyes narrowed. "I heard you moved to the Creek. Bad news travels fast. Hey, we can pick up right where we left off last year." His face darkened. "I also heard you have a team in the summer basketball league. I have a team too, and we're unstoppable. I'm going to enjoy grinding you into the hardwood."

Matt was so angry he couldn't speak for a moment. "We'll see who goes down, Beal. Our team knows how to handle a goon like you."

Beal scoffed. "You don't look like much of a threat to me. My team eats wimps like you for breakfast." He turned his attention back to Mary. "I haven't seen you before. If you're what the new crop of girls is like at Bragg Creek, I'm going to enjoy school a whole lot more than last time." He grinned at her with a mouth-ful of extremely white teeth.

Matt wondered if Beal's teeth were real. "Why don't you take a hike, Beal?" Matt said, wanting to let his fist check out those shiny white teeth.

"You know, Eagletail, I think I will. Of course, I have two good legs, which makes it a little easier." He laughed, making a noise like water gurgling in a sewer pipe.

Jazz walked over to him, her face a study in con-trolled fury. "If I were you, I'd listen to my brother and get lost. Go back to Loserville where you belong." Her eyes flashed.

"Look, John," Mary interrupted, trying to calm things down. "It is John, isn't it? I'm Mary," she smiled at him engagingly, "and I don't think this is the time or place for this, do you?"

Beal leered at her, his attention diverted from Matt and Jazz. "You name the right time and place and I'll be there, Gorgeous."

Mary blushed, a little flustered. "What I mean is, a guy in as obviously good shape as you are, well, it wouldn't look right if you picked a fight with a guy in a wheelchair, or even two guys in wheelchairs. They're no match for you. Why don't you wait until Matt is back on his feet to continue this discussion? That way you don't look like the bad guy."

Matt could see Mary's words working on the big

bully. He nodded his head at her.

"You might have something. I wouldn't even break a sweat taking both these wimps on." He started to move over beside her, but Mary casually kept Matt's wheelchair between herself and Beal.

"I think it's time you were leaving." Matt looked pointedly at the big teenager.

Beal ignored him, his attention focused on Mary. "What do you say I join you? I was going in to see . . ." he hesitated. "What is it we're going to see, *Mary*?" He emphasized her name as though they were already best friends.

"Sorry, I'm busy, John. I'm with my friends and we've made plans." She walked away from him and stood with Jazz.

"There's always room for one more," he said, eyeing Jazz.

Matt was furious. He could feel heat rising under his collar, but what could he do in this wheelchair? "You big, ignorant . . ." Matt started to say as he wheeled his chair forward toward Beal.

"You want a piece of me, Eagletail? Well, bring it on." The athletic teen moved toward Matt.

Matt's chair rolled into a rut on a grating and stuck. He felt humiliated as he tried in vain to free the stubborn wheel.

"This has been real interesting," Free Throw's calm voice made Beal's head snap around. "But I don't think either Mary or Jazz wants to join you. Now if you'll excuse us . . ."

"What have we here? Another broken-down wheelchair jockey friend of Eagletail's?" Beal asked, smirking.

"You'd be right about the friend part," Free Throw said calmly. He waved at someone coming down the steps behind Beal.

"Can I help you folks out?" a gentleman in a red vest and white Stetson cowboy hat asked. His nametag identified him as an official with the Stampede.

"Yes, please. My friends and I are looking for the wheelchair ramp so we can go see the photo exhibit. Can you direct us?" Free Throw smiled congenially at the Calgary Stampede Courtesy Cowboy.

"I'll do better than that. If you'll come with me, I'll show you folks how to get inside. You need to go around the corner to the wheelchair access."

Beal snarled at Matt. "This isn't over, Eagletail. We'll finish this on the court." He turned and disappeared back into the crowd on the midway.

Matt was shaking so hard, he could barely wheel his chair up the wide ramp once the helpful cowboy had freed it from the annoying grate. How had Free Throw remained so calm? Matt had wanted to punch Beal in the face, except he couldn't reach it from where he was now.

"You have to look at things a little differently from this altitude," Free Throw said as he moved up next to

Matt. "The guy was a jerk. Don't worry about it. I'm sure he was all talk, but it's never a good idea to pick a fight with a guy who's four feet taller than you are." And with that, he moved off and joined Jazz and Mary who were already heading toward the photo exhibit.

Matt watched him for a moment. Then, taking a deep breath, wheeled his chair a little faster to catch up. Free Throw was right. He'd been dumb to challenge Beal. What would have happened if he had punched Beal?

Matt suspected the answer. He'd have bled a lot.

★ ★ ★

The infield events at the Calgary Stampede were filled with horses, bulls, dust, and cowboys. Matt and Free Throw sat with his family in the section allocated for people with special needs. They had a great view of all the action.

Matt looked around at the noisy crowd that filled the grandstands. Thousands of people cheered each contestant as he took his turn in the afternoon's events. Everyone was dressed in riding boots and Stetson hats with enthusiastic cries of "Yaaaaahoo!" every time a cowboy finished his ride. It was impossible not to be caught up in the excitement.

"Wow! This is great! We don't have anything like the Calgary Stampede at home!" Free Throw exclaimed as he watched the saddle bronc riding. The big horse leapt and whirled, trying to buck off the cowboy, who stayed stubbornly glued to the saddle. Everyone cheered as the eight-second horn sounded, signifying the end of the bumpy ride.

"Man, I love those chaps the cowboys have on," Free Throw said, referring to the protective leather pants they wore over their blue jeans.

"I think the way he kept his hat on through the whole ride was pretty impressive," Matt said appreciatively.

There were a lot of other events, but the family was split on which was the most exciting.

Jazz thought the bull riding was definitely the scariest. "Look at how huge the bull is, and how puny the rider is," she said. "One stomp of a hoof and your dancing career is over!"

Matt shook his head. "No way! Calf roping is the most exciting. That cowboy has to come out of the chute at full throttle, then lasso a running calf, and get his horse to stop on a dime and not move, even though a two-hundred-pound calf is fighting to get free while he ties its feet together! Now that's entertainment!"

"Well, I'd rather go back on the carousel," Daisy said, folding her arms and sitting back in her seat. "I think the cowboys are mean."

"You liked the wild cow milking contest," her stepmother reminded her. "You thought that was funny."

Daisy giggled. "That's because those cowboys didn't

know milk comes from the supermarket, not those crazy cows they were chasing around."

"Well, my favourite is not till this evening," Matt's stepdad added. "I love the chucks."

"They are exciting," Matt's mom agreed. "In fact, going to the races was our first date." She smiled lovingly at her husband.

"What's *upchucks*?" Marigold asked, her face screwed up. "It sounds pretty gross."

"The *chuck wagon* races are where old-style wagons with canvas canopies, pulled by a team of horses, race against each other," Matt explained. "The wagons have out-riders who have to throw an old stove into the back, quickly run and jump on their waiting horses, and then everyone gallops for the finish. It's really exciting."

"I can hardly wait!" Free Throw said, catching Matt's enthusiasm.

"I think you'd make a great cowboy," Rosemary said, walking beside Free Throw's chair as they left the grandstand after the infield events and made their way to a food tent.

Matt was still having a little trouble negotiating with his chair. He marvelled at how Free Throw kept going, seemingly with no trouble at all. Matt's arms were tired and his shoulders ached from wheeling himself around all day. He pushed harder on the wheels, trying to keep up with the rest of the family without making the effort it took too obvious.

"Thanks, Rosie," Free Throw said. "But from what I saw today, I'll stick to something safer, like test pilot for experimental planes or daredevil motorcycle jumper."

Matt thought about their meeting with Beal. "You might find coaching for the Wildcats pretty exciting if our friend Beal carries out his plan to turn me into floor polish."

Free Throw's mouth set in a firm line. "No worries. I'm going to work on some special plays. He won't know what hit him."

Matt hoped he was right.

6 BACK IN THE GAME

Matt felt great as he left the doctor's office. His legs were a little shaky and he still had to be careful how and where he stepped until his full strength returned. He caught a glimpse of himself in a store window — he looked like someone who had just run a marathon as he favoured his extremely tender legs. The important thing was that he'd been given the go-ahead to start using them again. The muscles might still be stiff from being twisted like pretzels, but that was nothing a good game of basketball couldn't fix.

"You've grown two feet since I last saw you!" Free Throw said when Matt walked into the house. "A left one and a right one." He started chortling. "Pretty lame joke, huh?" He laughed out loud. "Come on Matt, lighten up. It's just a little wheelchair humour."

Matt frowned, and then decided if Free Throw could laugh, so could he. He smiled weakly at his friend. "I can hardly wait for Wednesday's game. The doc said to take it easy for a while, so I'd better enjoy tonight, because in two days, I'm playing basketball."

That evening, the family went for supper to Matt's grandparents on the Tsuu T'ina reserve. Free Throw really enjoyed the traditional meal of slow-cooked buffalo roast, bannock, and wild greens, plus Saskatoon pie for dessert.

"I think there may be some Tsuu T'ina in me," Free Throw said between bites. "I love this food." Matt's grandmother beamed appreciatively and heaped more meat on Free Throw's plate, complaining because no one else wanted fourths.

Matt looked around at his family and best friend. He had a lot to be grateful for, not the least of which was the simple ability to have walked up the steps to his grandmother's porch without help. The last week really made him stop and think.

★ ★ ★

The next day, as Matt sat relaxing in an easy chair, he revelled in how easily he could wiggle his toes. He could hardly wait to get back on the court.

"How are you doing, Honey Bear?" his mother asked as she came downstairs. Matt shook his head at the term of endearment his mom had used since he was a very little boy. He'd asked her not to say it in front of the geese, because, after all, he was the oldest, and somehow the name *Honey Bear* didn't sound very mature.

"I feel great, Mom. You know, I have a whole new respect for people who are physically challenged. My life is pretty simple compared with people who are disabled." Matt flexed his feet again.

"And something you tend to forget is that these folks also have all the everyday problems the rest of us have, so I'd say their coping skills are probably a notch higher." His mom nodded at him. "I hope you remember your experiences this past week the next time someone has a problem doing math, or opening a jar, or even putting a basketball through a hoop. We all have talents, just not the same ones, and you might not be able to see them because the wheelchair or the cane gets in the way. It's these many different gifts that makes all of us so interesting."

She spoke casually, but Matt knew her words were from the heart. She had a simple way of saying things that were important. He nodded at his mom. "I understand, Mom, and I promise I won't forget."

She moved around the family room, tidying and straightening almost unconsciously. "We can leave for the movie as soon as you're ready," she said cheerfully, then went back upstairs with two spoons and the empty peanut butter jar Marigold and Daisy had enjoyed as a snack.

Matt thought about his mom's words. His experience in the wheelchair had given him a new perspective about disabilities and he felt he understood a lot more about life than he used to. One thing was for sure: he'd never take his legs for granted again. He was a lucky guy.

To celebrate Matt's regained mobility, they had decided to go to a new movie that promised thrills, spills, and lots of action. Jazz had invited Mary again; Matt definitely liked having her around.

Precious trotted into the room and stared at him with unwavering brown eyes. "What do you want, Furball?" he asked the big white dog. The dog didn't answer, but kept staring at Matt. Finally, Matt couldn't stand it anymore and got up. Precious bounded to the door and stood looking over his shoulder, waiting.

"Okay, okay, I'm coming. Nothing I like better than being a doorman for a dog," he grumbled and went to let the hairy canine out. As he opened the door, Jazz called to him from the driveway.

"Great! You got my message." She walked toward Matt dribbling a basketball. "I sent Precious in to get you. Care to shoot a few hoops while we wait for Mary?" She grinned at her stepbrother.

Matt caught the ball she tossed to him. "You bet! I'm never too busy to show a struggling pupil how it's done." He spun the ball on the end of his finger. "Oh, and Jazz," he began a little hesitantly, "the other day when we ran into Beal at the Stampede, I wanted you to know I thought what you said was cool."

Jazz thought a moment. "Oh, you mean about him

being from Loserville? Beal's probably the mayor!"
She giggled.

Matt caught the ball and looked at her, tipping his
head self-consciously to one side. "No, I meant about the
brother part. I noticed." It had been the first time she'd
called him by that term instead of the usual *stepbrother.*

Now it was Jazz's turn to look self-conscious. "Yeah,
well, blood is thicker than water and besides, I kinda
think of you that way." They exchanged a look, and
then Matt turned his attention back to the basketball.

Suddenly noticing Free Throw sitting in the shade
beside the garage, he nodded. "You here to give Jazz
some pointers too?" he asked. "Be warned, she doesn't
take suggestions very well." Jazz punched him on the
arm as Matt tossed a long, high lob, which hit the backboard and popped back toward her.

"You're getting really good at those air balls. If I
ever want any pointers on them, I'll know who to ask."
She snagged the ball and, with a touch like velvet, sent
it home to nestle contentedly in the net.

"All right, Jasmine!" she said, and proceeded to do
her crazy victory dance. This wild wiggle walk, which
included waving her hands over her head, was what
Jazz did whenever she scored a basket.

Free Throw watched her, his eyes flashing with
laughter. "Very nice, Miss Eagletail-Thoreau, we'll be
in touch. Next!" He motioned for the next imaginary
dancer to enter.

Then Mary walked around the corner of the garage. "Hi, you guys," she said brightly.

Matt, Jazz, and Free Throw all broke up at her perfect timing. She wasn't alone, though — Noah was with her.

"I thought I'd hone my less-than-exemplary skills while you four are otherwise occupied at the theatre," he said with a serious voice.

"You mean you want to practice b-ball while we go the movies?" Matt asked.

"Precisely!" Noah agreed.

"Okay with me. Tomorrow's a big game." Matt was secretly glad the strange guy wasn't going with them.

"You know," Free Throw began. "I'm not really feeling up to a movie, Matt. You guys go ahead without me. I'm going to hang here." He rested his hand on his legs and Matt nodded.

"Sure, old buddy, no problem." He hoped Free Throw was okay. He'd become so used to thinking of him as a normal guy that he now found himself forgetting Free Throw might not always be able to keep up. After all, he wasn't made of steel just because he acted like it.

The three friends clambered into the van with Matt's mom and the geese, who were going to see a new Disney epic, and headed off to the movies. Matt had worn a new sweatshirt with the logos of NBA teams all over it. He liked the bright colours and thought the collar of the white shirt he wore underneath made him look more dressed up — not that this was a date or anything. He simply wanted to look nice.

The ride home was noisy with the twins discussing every detail of the kids' movie they'd seen. Violet loved the extravagant costumes and Daisy liked the talking dog, but — she assured Jazz — not as much as Precious, even if Precious couldn't talk, not really. Matt had sat beside Mary and had been acutely aware of her through the whole of their movie. She'd even smiled at him a couple of times and this had made his heart start pumping faster.

Everyone stormed into the house when they got home. It went from quiet and peaceful to noisy and boisterous in less than two seconds. Matt went to find Free Throw to tell him about the movie, but he wasn't in their room. Then he heard a familiar sound outside. He looked out the backdoor window and stared. There was Noah, shooting baskets, or at least trying to shoot baskets. But that wasn't the part that made Matt stare in disbelief. Matt slowly pushed open the door and walked out to where the uncoordinated astronomer was practising.

He wasn't practising alone.

"Okay, bend your wrist back until you can see wrinkles. Now, let the ball roll off your fingertips like you were waving goodbye to it. Concentrate on the rim through the whole shot." Free Throw watched

Noah as he sent the ball sailing toward the backboard. *Swish!* Nothing but net.

"Astounding!" Noah yelled ecstatically.

Free Throw wheeled up and snagged the ball, then headed back across the court, turned, and with one hand, sent the ball sailing back toward the basket. The ball kissed the backboard, and then sank gently into the net. It was a thing of beauty!

"Way to go, Free Throw!" Matt said excitedly. He'd never seen Free Throw do anything but *hold* a basketball. But now, here he was sinking baskets like he'd been doing it all his life.

"And Noah," Free Throw said casually, gliding over to grab the ball.

"What?" Matt asked, confused.

"And Noah. You didn't congratulate Noah on a perfectly executed shot," Free Throw corrected Matt, as if his shooting hoops was an everyday occurrence and it was Noah who'd done something extraordinary. Come to think of it, Matt thought, Noah had!

"Oh, yeah, nice shooting, Noah," Matt added, then turned back to Free Throw before Noah had a chance to say anything. "Free Throw, what's going on? How come you're playing ball? Why didn't you tell me you were going to do this?" he asked in a rush.

Free Throw tossed Noah the ball. "Noah, could you practise the layup drill I showed you?"

"I will consider that lofty challenge my personal

goal," Noah said, trying to dribble the ball in the direction of the net.

Free Throw wheeled over to talk to Matt. "Let's go down to the end of the driveway."

When they got to the bottom of the drive, Free Throw stopped. Holding up his hand to prevent Matt from saying anything, he began his explanation. "It's like this. I had no choice but to help Noah with his game. This guy obviously was thrilled at being allowed on the team, no matter how little actual court time he got, but he needed some help if he was ever going to be played. Mary tries, but I don't think Nigel encourages him to go out for sports, so I thought I'd step in and help out. Noah's important. I can shelve my own problems while I give him a few tips." He pushed his hair back off his forehead.

Matt understood what it had taken for Free Throw to play ball again. He'd told Matt he hadn't been on a court since the accident. He'd said he would go back, just not now, and *now* had turned from months into years.

"Besides, I've come up with some new plays for tomorrow's game, and I needed to test them out with someone." He smiled sheepishly at Matt. "I know what it's like to be singled out because you're different. You probably do too, Matt. Being short and ugly, you're not typical basketball material, but still, you got a chance to show you can play despite your shortcomings." He smiled at his joke. "All I want is for Noah to have a chance. He'll probably never make an all-star, but he really wants to play. This is a summer league, no one's NBA career is on the line, so I thought I'd help Noah be the best player he can be for one summer." He sat back in his chair and waited.

Matt instantly saw the big picture. Free Throw was right. They would both go on with basketball and they'd succeed, but this might be Noah's only chance to experience the thrill of playing the game of games. Matt sighed. It was so simple when you put it like that. They started back up the driveway.

"You know something, Free Throw?" Matt said, squinting into the sun as he walked.

"What?" his friend asked, concentrating on positioning his hands exactly right on the wheels as he moved beside Matt.

"When you're a coach in the NBA, you won't ever have to worry about your team losing a championship," Matt said, looking out over the freshly-mowed lawn.

"How do you figure that?" Free Throw asked, not looking at Matt.

"Give them a song and dance like the one you just laid on me, and it's in the bag!" Matt grinned at his friend.

"Yup," Free Throw said, smiling back.

They finished walking back to where Noah waited with the basketball firmly clasped in his hands.

7 THE MEAN MACHINE

Game day is always exciting, but for Matt, today was really special. He was back. He warmed up on the court, loosening his muscles and testing his legs. They were playing a team called the Mean Machine and Matt had heard they were good. In fact, they'd never lost a game. He shrugged as he thought of this statistic. No big deal. After today, the Machine would have their first loss to add to the stats.

Noah, his uniform hanging loosely on his tall, angular frame, came in jogging and waving to the crowd, who didn't seem to notice him at all. "It's time for the indomitable Wildcats to perform their feats of athletic prowess and basketball wonder-working sorcery," he said, adjusting his glasses on his long, thin nose with a grand wave of his hand.

Jimmy Big Bear looked at him like he wasn't sure which planet Noah had dropped in from. Noah shook each of the Wildcats' hands, then casually assumed his usual position on the bench. Tony, the power forward, looked over at Cory, who would play starting centre. Cory shrugged his shoulders. "Don't look at me, Tony. I've got no clue what he said."

Free Throw shook his head. "Hey, I'm American. I don't speak your strange Canadian dialect." He wheeled his chair over to Noah and handed him a thick elastic strap. "It's for your glasses, so they don't slip in the heat of battle." He smiled at the awkward teenager who sat staring at the strap.

Noah held the band like he was getting a gift from the gods. "You have no idea how this simple gesture of confidence touches me. I shall wear my elastic strap like a badge of honour. Thank you, Coach Free Throw."

Free Throw nodded. "No problemo."

Matt noticed Nigel was sitting on the edge of the bench, tying his court shoes, and seemed not to have even noticed what the rest of the team was doing. The ref's whistle brought the two teams to the jump circle at centre court. Matt started walking to his position as point guard, but saw Nigel heading out onto the court too.

"I'm starting today, Nigel. We can switch off a little later." Matt pulled himself up, trying to look taller next to the athletic boy.

"You should be playing sixth man, Matt, not starting lineup," Nigel looked pointedly at Matt's legs. "Why don't you go sit this round out and you can substitute when someone needs a break?"

Matt wondered if Nigel was truly concerned for

his legs. If he was, he could have phrased his suggestion better. It wouldn't have mattered to Matt, though. Today he was playing. "Not according to the coach. You can go talk to him." He nodded toward Free Throw.

"Nigel, over here!" Free Throw called. "You're in next round." Nigel's face went red as he returned to the bench to sit beside his older brother.

Matt took his place at the jump circle. Part of his job being point guard would be to direct the team while on the floor.

As he glanced around at the players readying themselves for the first tipoff of the game, his eyes met and locked with a familiar enemy. It was John Beal. Matt stared at the big ball player in surprise.

Beal played for the Mean Machine! He nodded at Matt and grinned, showing his perfectly aligned, dazzlingly white teeth that automatically made Matt's hand twitch into a fist.

"Hey, you got rid of your training wheels, Eagletail. I guess you think that makes you a match for me." His eyes narrowed. "Better think again. This is going to be like taking candy from a baby!"

Matt ignored the comment. He hoped Free Throw's new plays worked as well as the young coach thought they would. They were going to need an edge — a big one.

Cory tipped the ball to Matt who grabbed it, deked under the arm of the man covering him, and streaked to the basket. He could hear the other players closing behind him as he went in for an uncontested layup. Ah, the element of surprise! No one expected him to be able to jump the way he did or move as fast as he did. Two points, easy as that, Matt thought, as he headed back downcourt. He could feel Beal glaring at him.

"Nice shot, Point Guard," Free Throw called.

Matt gave a signal to the rest of the team, letting them know they were going to use one of Free Throw's new plays. The team set up and moved out toward the oncoming Mean Machine. The play depended on everyone moving lightning-fast with precision passing. The first step was to force a turnover. Jimmy Big Bear smiled. This was his speciality. He moved in front of the Machine player who was dribbling through traffic. His size alone made other players look twice.

A split second's hesitation was all Jimmy needed. He snatched the ball away and before any Machine players could react, he snapped it to Matt, who turned and bounce passed it to Cory, who chest passed to Tony, who flipped one to Ron. The ball was well down the court by now and Ron had an easy layup.

Beal was furious as he yelled at his teammates to close up the gap. They started back downcourt again, but another of Free Throw's magic plays gave the Wildcats an additional two points. With a comfortable lead as a cushion, Free Throw signalled for a substitution. Matt, Ron, and Cory came off and Nigel, Jazz, and Mary went in.

"Oh look, the Wildcats have *girls* on their team," Beal said sarcastically. "What's the matter, couldn't find enough *men*?"

"Beal, why don't you shut up and try to play some decent ball for a change?" Jazz snapped back.

Beal's eyes narrowed and Matt could feel his anger right across the court.

"Close up, close up," Nigel called as a big hole opened in the Wildcats' defence. Jimmy moved to cover two oncoming Machine men until the defence tightened up.

"Gerry, over here," Beal called as he sped toward the basket. He snagged a nice chest pass and headed straight for Nigel. Nigel held his ground, waiting for the big player to come to him. Beal barrelled down at him like a tank, but Nigel wasn't going to move. Not able to force Nigel to retreat and with Wildcats closing in on both sides, Beal stopped. He had to choose from a risky cross-court pass or take the shot himself. He readied himself and went up for a jumpshot. He was too far out and the ball clanged harmlessly against the backboard before bouncing back into the crowd of players waiting beneath the basket. Beal shook his head as he ran to an open spot, hoping for another pass.

"Nigel did okay. Beal's a hard guy to stop," Matt said, complimenting Nigel.

Free Throw nodded. "He's supposed to put Operation Sidekick into play here. Let's see if he can follow orders."

Jimmy out-muscled and outmanoeuvred the other players to grab the rebound. He was what teachers called *assertive.*

Jazz and Larry were already heading back toward the Mean Machine's basket. Beal's team had Jimmy covered, but with a quick pivot, he opened enough of a hole to fire a pass to Jazz.

Jazz caught it, turned, and headed downcourt with a crowd of players closing fast. Mary dropped back and ran interference with several of the Machine players who didn't seem to know how to deal with the small whirlwind of a player. Nigel set a pick between Jazz and the oncoming players.

"Larry, coming at you!" Jazz called, and tossed a long baseball pass. Larry, out in the clear, turned and took the ball home for another two points.

This was going to be a walk in the park, Matt thought as he watched, ecstatic at the Wildcats' growing lead.

But on the next play, while the Wildcats were breaking a particularly nasty press, Larry suddenly took a hard nose-dive onto the floor. He fell awkwardly and twisted his knee as he landed. No one saw what happened, but Matt noticed the satisfied smirk on the player closest to Larry. It was Beal.

Larry hobbled off the floor. He sat heavily on the bench as Free Throw, with an assortment of elastic bandages and cold packs for exactly such an occasion, checked out the wounded player's knee.

The Wildcats' momentum seemed to slow down. A couple of plays later, Matt was back on the floor trying to help Tony trap a Machine player. The play went wrong when Nigel went for a hole instead of sticking to the plan and the ball-handler broke out, passed to a teammate, and the Machine had their first two points.

Free Throw signalled for a time out to be called and motioned Mary over to the bench. Matt couldn't believe his eyes when he saw Noah come jogging onto the court with his mile-wide grin. *He* was the Wildcats' substitute shooting guard?

Beal took one look at Noah and began laughing. "And I thought you guys were scraping the bottom of the barrel when you sent the girls out to play! This game is in the bag!" he snorted, as the Mean Machine got ready for the next play.

"Don't be so sure, you insignificant little gnat!" Noah said bravely as he took his place in the lineup.

Matt exchanged a surprised look with Jimmy.

"Go get 'em, Tiger Blake," Jimmy chuckled.

Matt looked over toward the bench and got a nod from Free Throw.

"Cory, you and Jimmy get ready to receive one of *Tiger's bullet passes.* Tony and I will screen for you," Matt called loudly.

The Mean Machine looked from one player to another, unsure if what they heard was true. Noah didn't look like he could toss a ball from one hand to the other, let alone a bullet pass downcourt.

"Watch him, watch him," Beal growled, now a little unsure himself.

The second the ball was in play, Beal's teammates swarmed Noah, effectively stopping him from receiving the ball. This was okay with Matt, because he and Tony had a play of their own. A quick pump fake and a pivot, followed by a pass, and Tony was on his way for a beautiful hassle-free layup.

Beal's face was like a threatening thundercloud. He gave a couple of signals to his teammates and suddenly, it was like playing Australian rugby. The Wildcats were taking elbow jabs, shots to the knees, and once, Matt was *accidentally* sent careening into a couple of chairs that were set up at courtside. Beal happened to be the closest player again. His team started scoring baskets, a lot of them. The refs caught some of what was going on, but they missed a lot. The Wildcats began having passes picked off and were slowing down from the constant dirty play.

Jazz was flying downcourt on a breakaway, when Beal seemed to stumble and fall right in front of her. Jazz had no time to avoid hitting him and went down hard. She had wicked floor burns on her legs when she got up.

"You jerk! You did that on purpose!" she yelled at Beal who was getting to his feet.

"What's the matter? Game too tough for a wimpy

little girl?" he said sarcastically. "Besides, it was an accident. I tripped," he gurgled to himself as Jazz limped to the bench, cursing under her breath.

On the next play, Matt was ready. When Beal tried to come around him, Matt stuck his elbow out far enough to catch the big teen in the stomach. Matt heard the wind go out of his opponent.

"I'll get you for that, Eagletail," he snarled.

"This is between you and me, Beal. Leave my sister out of it." Matt dodged around the big player and headed downcourt.

Beal managed to intercept a pass, turned and swept back toward the waiting basket. Matt was right on his heels. As he got within shooting range, Beal stopped dead on the court. Matt had expected him to go all the way in for a layup and was unprepared. He ran right into the back of Beal and went sprawling on the floor. He lay still for a minute, the wind knocked out of him.

Beal took his shot and it was good. Matt closed his eyes, trying to get his breath back.

"I told you I'd grind you into the hardwood, Eagletail," Beal growled as he walked past Matt lying on the cold floor.

The score was now tied. Free Throw called for a time out and Matt walked slowly off the court.

"Guys, I've got a play that will win this game for us. It's one Matt and I talked about." He quickly explained his newest strategy to the tired players.

"I think I should go in for Matt," Nigel said after he'd heard the play. "He's not looking too good."

Matt's head whipped around. His eyes shot sparks. "I'm fine. This is a play I helped develop, Nigel. Since it's our last chance to pull a win out of the bag, I think I'd better jockey this one."

"I think I could handle one play," Nigel snidely persisted.

"Next time," Free Throw said, siding with Matt.

Nigel glanced around at the other Wildcats. Their faces were stony. "Sure," he said. "Next time. The win's the important thing."

"All right! That's the spirit!" Free Throw said, defusing the situation. "Now go show the Machine how to play basketball!"

When the Wildcats hit the floor they were running on pure adrenalin. The game moved up a notch in intensity. Matt and the Wildcats suddenly owned the court. They had the Machine players running for a ball which was always an arm's length out of their reach. They moved down the court like they'd invented the game. When Matt finally went in for his amazing reverse layup, the crowd was already on its feet cheering the Wildcats' victory. The sight and sound of the ball falling through the net was exactly what Matt needed. Two points and a Wildcat win!

He was ecstatic! The Wildcats had beaten Beal and his goons! He had beaten Beal. If they could beat the

Machine, they could beat anyone.

Matt watched as Beal and the Machine left. Some of the players angrily picked up their equipment, then stormed off the floor, while others kept looking over at the Wildcats' bench as though they couldn't believe they'd lost to a team that had short guys, girls, and geeks playing for them. Beal looked like he wanted to rip something up and stuff it into a garbage bin.

It had been a tough game. Three Machine players had been fouled out and most of the Wildcats were wearing bandages or bruises. The 'Cats didn't seem to mind at all. Free Throw was hailed the hero of the game.

"You deserve all the credit for this win, old buddy," Matt said enthusiastically. "We couldn't have done it without your plays."

"Consider it a warm-up for the tournament," Free Throw said, grinning.

The celebration at the Mountain Bistro, the Wildcats' favourite pizza hangout, was noisier and louder than it had ever been. Confident boasts and forecasted victories dominated the table talk. Everyone felt the Wildcats were going all the way.

8 LOSING IS ALWAYS TOUGH

Over the next couple of weeks, the Wildcats continued to play and win, thanks to Free Throw's ingenious plays and the team's confident attitude. They worked hard and were moving up in the standings. Matt checked the play schedule.

"Oh, great. We play the Mean Machine three more times before the finals. We could end up forfeiting because of lack of players due to serious breakage," he said, shaking his head.

"When's the next Machine game?" Jazz asked, as she lay back on the family room couch listening as Matt and Free Throw discussed strategy.

Matt made a face. "Saturday."

Mary, who was relaxing in an easy chair, looked over at him. "Great. We've got their number. We'll beat them again. I think we should have a practice and go over Free Throw's latest plays." Jazz, Free Throw, and Matt all agreed with her.

The team got together and practised until everyone

had all of Free Throw's new plays down pat.

"These are the trickiest yet!" Ron said, tossing the ball to Larry.

Matt had to agree. The plays were dynamite! "We'll clean up with these!" he agreed. "Great job, Free Throw!"

Free Throw and Jazz were practising a pump fake drill with Noah.

"They're like notes on a page, it's you virtuosos who turn them into a moving symphony!" Free Throw replied modestly, using some of Noah's flowery prose.

Everyone was feeling confident as they broke up and left for home. They'd beaten the Machine before and they'd beat them again.

★ ★ ★

The Wildcats were all feeling great on Saturday as they suited up for the game. Free Throw had gone over all the plays and was sure the win was in the bag.

Matt walked out onto the floor and Beal was waiting at the jump circle for him.

"You're a sucker for punishment, Eagletail," Beal said confidently.

"Big talk, Beal. I guess you need another lesson," Matt said, controlling his temper.

Beal snorted and turned away from Matt.

The Wildcats set up for the opening play of the game. Jimmy and Tony were the starting forwards,

Cory was centre, and Matt and Jazz were guards. Cory nodded at Jazz. She would take the tipoff and snap a bounce pass to Jimmy as Tony set up a screen. Jimmy would then pass to Cory, who would be downcourt. He'd go in for the layup. Simple.

From the second Cory tipped the ball to Jazz, it was as if the Machine knew who to cover and what was coming. None of Beal's men even attempted to guard Matt. They concentrated on the players who were involved in the play. It was an uncanny coincidence. It was also two points for the Machine as they cut the play off, stole the ball, and went for the Wildcats' net.

A couple of unsuccessful plays later, Free Throw had called for an *I-formation* play to which he'd added a little magic. This play is particularly good for throwing off the defence, as it's hard for them to pick up their assigned offensive players. With a Free Throw twist, it should have been surefire.

Should have been. The play was simple. It involved everyone moving quickly to a pre-assigned spot. Mary, who was inbounding the ball, would pass to Larry, who was closest to her at the baseline. He'd pump fake to Nigel, who would have moved toward the net, drawing the defence with him. Then Larry would pass to Matt, who'd go up for a clean jumpshot from an undefended position near the three-point arc. No problem.

Nigel waited to be swarmed, except the Machine headed straight for Matt, who was farthest from the basket and should have been left open. Beal stayed to cover Nigel, who couldn't seem to shake him despite some really impressive footwork. Larry, unable to pass to Matt, had no choice but to try to make his way through traffic to get to a better scoring position. The whole play collapsed.

Play after play was demolished. The 'Cats couldn't seem to get anything going. Free Throw tried every trick in his book, but the Machine knew where to be to finish the play before it got started. The team was losing ground and no one seemed able to stop it.

"This is nuts! We can't get close to these guys," Jazz complained, coming off the floor after a particularly gruelling shift. "It's like they know what we're going to do before we even do it!" She grabbed her towel from the bench.

"Are we telegraphing our plays somehow, Matt?" Mary asked, watching the carnage on the floor.

Matt shook his head. "No, you guys are doing everything right. I don't understand it."

Free Throw was frantically going through his playbook to try and find something that might get the Wildcats back on track. "I'll have to come up with some new plays before the next game against these guys or we're sunk," he said, discouraged.

Jazz and Mary stood and watched. Matt was so frustrated he paced up and down muttering to himself as he tried to figure out what was happening on the floor. By three-quarter time, the score was a disappointing

54–28 for the Machine.

It got worse. By the time the final buzzer sounded, the score was 62–30. The worst part was that Beal and his goons hadn't even used their usual grind-them-into-dust style of play. They had outmanoeuvred the 'Cats at every turn.

"It's only one bad game," Jazz said as they grabbed their gear.

"Don't worry," Mary said confidently. "We'll get them next time." She smiled at Matt and it almost made up for the humiliating loss.

But a week later, the Wildcats went down to the Mean Machine in another demoralizing defeat. The same grim scenario played out with the Machine able to out-think the 'Cats at every turn.

"You know it's bad when Beal and his buddies don't even have to collect fouls to win," Jimmy grumbled as he downed the last of his bottled water following the losing game.

"It's a good thing there were no scouts in the audience today," Nigel commented, almost cheerily. "It wouldn't have done my pro career any good to be seen playing for this team."

Matt whirled on him, ready to cut him down, but decided not to turn this into a fight. Everyone was tired and frustrated. It wasn't so much what Nigel said as the way he said it. Matt knew Nigel felt smug about the fact that this was only a summer league. In the fall, he'd be going back to the team in Calgary and more serious ball, but he could at least pretend he liked the 'Cats, Matt thought. After all, he was playing for them.

He nodded curtly at Nigel. "Yeah, we're here for the fun too." Matt could hear the sarcasm in his voice and only partially regretted his tone.

★ ★ ★

The team tried to put the losses behind them. They had to play the Machine once more before the finals, and Matt hoped that game would be different. They were doing okay against the rest of the league, but couldn't seem to get back on track with the Machine.

"We've got to go shopping in Bragg Creek this afternoon," Matt announced early one Friday morning.

"Sure, why?" Free Throw asked, pulling on a royal purple T-shirt with the logo of the LA Lakers emblazoned in bright gold letters.

"Because today's the twins' birthdays and I have to get them birthday presents," Matt explained.

"That's cool. Which twins?" Free Throw asked, wrestling to pull the shirt down behind his back.

Matt chuckled. "All of them!"

That afternoon, Matt, Free Throw, Jazz, and Mary walked into Bragg Creek to try and find something great for both sets of twins, whose birthdays were all on the same day.

"I don't want to get them the same thing but in different colours, which is what everyone does for identical twins. I want to get each twin their own present," Matt said as they went into nearly every store in the small town.

The four friends were coming out of one of the many gift shops they were exploring when Mary put her hand on Matt's arm. "Look who else is shopping," she said, nodding to a tall boy crossing the street. Matt looked in the direction she'd indicated. It was Beal. He felt his temper rise instantly. The guy was about as welcome as ants at a picnic.

"Yuck!" Jazz said, making a face. "Let's go this way," she nodded her head in the opposite direction. "I don't want to spoil my day."

As the four watched, Beal waved to someone sitting on a bench in the small park that bordered the shopping plaza. When the big teen disappeared into the grove of pines, Matt relaxed. "Good riddance," he said, returning to his original good humour. "Okay, where to next on our tour of every store in Bragg Creek?" he asked Jazz and Mary.

"I've got a great idea what to get all the twins and I know they'll love it," Jazz said confidently. "Mary and I are going to the hardware store. We'll meet you back here in twenty minutes."

Matt and Free Throw had finished their shopping and were patiently waiting for the girls when Jazz and

Mary came running across the parking lot. Their faces were flushed and Jazz looked like a cat who'd eaten a canary. She must have some great presents, Matt thought, stuffing his own into his knapsack.

"Sorry we're late," Jazz said breathlessly. "We got held up." She grinned at Matt and Free Throw. "You know, this has been a really great shopping trip. You never know what little surprises you'll run across," she said obscurely.

Matt gave her a curious glance. "Like what?" he asked suspiciously.

"Well, if we told you, it wouldn't be a surprise, would it?" Jazz said cryptically.

"We'd better get going if we're going to make the party," Mary said. A look passed between her and Jazz.

Jazz nodded her head almost imperceptibly, and then her face brightened. "Double chocolate chunk cake, here we come!" she said grinning. "I can hardly wait. I hope Mom made enough for seconds."

"Count me in," Matt agreed, thinking of his mom's delicious dessert. "All we have to do is survive an afternoon with about a thousand little kids screaming and yelling. I think the twins have invited every one of their friends within a twenty kilometre radius!" Matt sighed as they headed home.

★ ★ ★

The party was definitely a success. There seemed to be an endless stream of children being dropped off and picked up all afternoon. Games were played, with Precious watching over the children as though they were his loyal subjects and he was their canine king.

"Wow, will you get a load of this place!" Matt exclaimed appreciatively as he and Free Throw joined the festivities under the shade of the tall pines in the backyard. "Mom must have been very busy decorating while we were gone."

He and Free Throw stared. There were brilliantly coloured streamers draped in all the trees, and tiny white lights twinkled merrily among the branches. Bright balloons flew from the veranda, adding to the general birthday atmosphere as children in party hats ran laughing between the tables of treats that were set up.

Free Throw whistled softly. "Your mom really knows how to throw a shindig."

For the next couple of hours the entire family joined in playing games to the delight of the children, who had never seen adults play pin-the-tail-on-the-donkey or hide-and-seek.

As pieces of the rich chocolate cake were passed out, the twins opened their birthday presents. Each brightly wrapped gift was thoroughly *oohed* and *ahhed* over as the girls delighted in their treasures.

The gift Matt had given Daisy was particularly interesting.

"It's pretty, Matty. What is it?" Daisy asked, holding up the strange-looking gift.

"Oh my goodness!" Matt's mom exclaimed. "What a beautiful dream catcher! Matt, wherever did you find it?" she asked.

"At Sun Dance in Bragg Creek. There's lots of cool stuff." Matt went on to explain the Indian legend of the dream catcher to Daisy. The woven circle of twigs had a web with an opening in the centre and when you slept at night, the web caught all the bad dreams and only allowed the good ones through the opening. In the morning, the bright sunshine burnt up all the bad dreams.

"This is great because I've started a really scary new book and I need protection. Thanks, Matty." She smiled at her stepbrother.

The ongoing competition between Rosemary and Violet for Free Throw's attention became evident when it came time for Rosemary to open Free Throw's gift. She picked up her present from Free Throw and walked over to him to open it.

"Jeez and crackers!" Rosemary said dramatically when she saw the book on Rocky Mountain wildflowers. "This is wonderful, absolutely the best, I've never seen anything like it! How can I thank you?" She shot Violet a look loaded with victory, then, with a theatrical flourish, gave Free Throw a big kiss on the cheek.

Free Throw went scarlet. Violet turned purple. Matt began laughing. "That's two points for Rosie!" he said, holding up two fingers. Rosemary smiled innocently at Violet who was positively fuming.

It was a birthday party to remember.

Later, when the party had finally wound down, Free Throw and Matt were sitting on the veranda relaxing when they spied Jazz and Mary coming back from a walk with Precious.

Matt could see they were in an animated discussion about something. "Looks like the girls are discussing some controversial subject again, like which actor they like best." He shook his head.

Suddenly, Mary began waving her arms and yelling at Jazz. Jazz responded by pointing her finger at Mary and yelling back.

"Uh-oh. Looks like world war three has broken out," Free Throw warned as he watched the angry girls.

"Man, they're really going at it. Maybe we ought to go down there and break it up before they start hitting each other," Matt suggested. Suddenly, Mary stalked off and Jazz stormed back up to the house. Matt heard the door slam as she came inside.

"This ought to be good," he warned Free Throw. "Remember, no matter what we say, we'll be wrong, so my advice is," he grinned at his friend, "don't say anything. Just nod your head sympathetically."

Jazz burst out of the door and flopped onto the edge of the swing beside Matt. She was so angry she was practically vibrating.

"Of all the rotten . . ." Then she turned on Matt. "I don't want to talk about it." She sat back in the swing, her arms crossed in a very definite statement.

"Okay," was all Matt said.

"For your information, Matthew Eagletail-Thoreau, this is mostly your fault," Jazz fumed. "*Your* friend Mary Blake is a Canadian Benedict Arnold. Do you know what she told me? She said your attitude toward Beal is out of line and not fair. Just because his team can beat the Wildcats doesn't mean he's bad or totally evil. He's playing to win and there's nothing wrong with that. Mary said she really wants to win this tournament so Nigel will take her basketball seriously, but every time the 'Cats go out on the floor against the Machine, they look like a bunch of rank amateurs." She took a breath.

"You're saying Mary thinks Beal hasn't done anything wrong?" Matt asked incredulously.

"Well, she said he plays an aggressive style of ball, but that's okay," Jazz said.

"Aggressive?" Free Throw's eyes widened. "If that's aggressive, I'd hate to see him if he ever got really out of control."

Matt looked at Free Throw and shrugged. He didn't know what to say. This was something really unexpected. Matt decided he had no choice. He'd better talk to Mary and find out what was going on.

9 PLAYING FOR THE WRONG TEAM

Matt tossed and turned that night, thinking about Mary. He decided to see her first thing in the morning and straighten this whole thing out. He had to make her see that Beal's methods were wrong and were hurting the game. Finally, exhausted, he went to sleep with a plan.

The next morning Matt was up early. It was Saturday and he knew Mary always helped her mother out at the farmers market in Bragg Creek. He could talk to her there. Dressing as quietly as possible and slipping out of his room silently so he wouldn't wake Free Throw, Matt was busy putting his shoes on when a faint noise made him spin around. It was only Precious. The big dog must have heard him and come to see what was up.

"I'm going to talk to Mary," he whispered to the dog. "I'll be back before breakfast." Precious sat and lifted a paw, laying it on Matt's arm. "No, you can't come. You'll only be a pest," he said softly as he pushed the dog's paw off his arm.

"What about me? If I promise not to be a pest, can

I come?" Free Throw asked from behind Matt. Matt turned to see his friend already dressed and obviously planning on accompanying him. Apparently, no one was going anywhere alone this morning.

"Sure," Matt said, then saw the dog's mournful expression. "Okay, you can come too, Precious. Let me get your leash."

The three set out down the hill toward Bragg Creek with Precious happily enjoying the fresh early-morning smells along the path. The farmers market was always busy with tourists and locals buying vegetables and handicrafts. Mary's mom supplied the world's best clover honey, which Matt loved. Thinking about it made him wish he'd eaten breakfast before setting out on this expedition.

When they arrived at the market, Matt saw Mary helping her mother set up their booth. Her brothers were also there, unloading boxes from Mrs. Blake's car. Noah waved when he saw Matt, but Nigel ignored him.

"You and Precious can look around. I'll be right back," Matt told Free Throw, handing him the dog's leash as he headed toward the brightly-coloured booth.

Matt stood quietly for a moment, and then cleared his throat. "Good morning, Mrs. Blake. May I speak with Mary for a minute?"

Mary turned and saw him. "It's okay, Mom. I'll talk to him." Mary put down the jars of honey she was arranging and walked over to Matt.

She crossed her arms, staring him straight in the eye. "Matt, if this is about yesterday, you can save your breath. I think you've been unfair to John because he keeps beating the Wildcats."

Matt noted the use of Beal's first name. It didn't bode well for the rest of his speech. She looked at him and he suddenly felt his throat go tight. "Look, Beal can play ball, I'll give him that," Matt conceded, trying to defuse the situation. "But he also plays a dirty game. I know it and you know it too, Mary."

"Matt, how can you be so unfair? In the last game, the Wildcats took as many fouls as the Machine, so you can't say they won because they beat us up on the court." She waited for him to deny this.

"You're right," Matt agreed. "I don't know how Beal is able to figure out our strategy and cut us off at every turn, but I'm willing to bet if we ever start winning again, he'll go back to his old style, which is cheap shots and dirty play."

Mary shook her head. "You're just jealous. You haven't liked John ever since he beat you when you played for the Warriors." He saw her look over at her mother's booth. "My brothers are finished unloading the honey from the car. I have to go help my mom."

Matt reached out and gently touched her arm. "All I'm asking is for you to think about Beal. A leopard never changes his spots, remember that."

She pulled her arm away and strode back to the booth.

Matt slowly walked over to where Free Throw and Precious waited at a corn stand, trying to be inconspicuous.

Free Throw had a big bag of fresh corn sitting on his lap. "I had to do something while I waited," he explained when Matt glanced curiously at the overflowing bag. "Didn't go so well, huh?"

"You could say that," Matt agreed, taking Precious's leash back but not looking at Free Throw. He didn't talk much for the rest of the walk home.

★ ★ ★

Mary missed the next couple of practices and Matt wasn't able to contact her on the phone. When questioned, Noah was at a loss and Nigel said not to worry, they didn't need her. Some close-knit family, Matt thought, when neither brother could explain her absence. Jazz hadn't said much about Mary's missing practice either. Once, Matt had heard Jazz on the phone giggling, and he'd thought she was talking to Mary and everything had been straightened out, but at the next practice, Mary still hadn't shown up.

The Wildcats were scheduled to meet the Mean Machine tomorrow for the final game before the big tournament and Matt intended to win that game. The team had worked really hard on practising Free Throw's new plays and everyone was confident that this time, they had the Machine.

Matt sat on the couch in the family room thinking gloomy thoughts. A lot of things were going badly in his life. He felt like he had no control. His team was on a losing streak with the Mean Machine, Beal hated his guts and was out to pulverize him, and now Mary thought he was an unfair jerk and had dropped out of his life. The last, but not least, piece of bad news had come from Free Throw this morning. He'd told Matt he was going to have to go home right after the big tournament next week.

Matt took a deep breath and exhaled loudly. No sense sitting here collecting dust, he thought. Trying to shake off the depressed feelings, Matt went outside to join Free Throw and Noah, who had come over to practise his amazing feats of basketball prowess.

"Come on, Point Guard, take your best shot. It will cheer you up!" Free Throw promised.

Matt nodded and caught the ball Free Throw tossed him. "Your first kick at the cat."

He'd just taken his shot when Matt heard Precious, whom he'd left napping contentedly on the couch, start scratching at the door and whining to get out.

"He probably woke up and discovered Jazz went to the schoolyard to shoot hoops without him," Matt said, going to the door. The big dog surged out and ran toward the path that led to the schoolyard.

"Here comes Jazz now," Free Throw said, looking

down the hill in the direction Precious had run. As she got closer, Matt noticed one of her knees was freshly skinned and blood was trickling down onto her white sport sock. He also noticed one other important thing — she didn't have his basketball with her. This instantly annoyed Matt. First, it was his favourite ball, which he'd been given when he'd become captain of the Tsuu T'ina Warriors, and second, she'd promised to take care of it.

"What happened to you?" Matt asked as she stormed up to them.

"I had a little problem at the school ball court," she said angrily.

"What kind of problem?" Matt asked.

Jazz slid her back down the side of the garage and sat in the cool shade. "I sort of lost your basketball," she said evasively.

"What?" Matt's tone was a little too sharp. "I mean, what happened, Jazz? That ball meant a lot to me."

"I know, Hotshot. I didn't do it on purpose," she said defensively.

Matt sighed. This was like pulling hen's teeth. "Okay, how did you do it?" he asked in his sweetest, but obviously end-of-limited-patience voice.

"You don't want to know." She gingerly touched her knee, which was still bleeding.

Free Throw eyed the large scrape. "You should put something on that," he offered helpfully.

"After she tells me what happened to my basketball,"

Matt scowled at Free Throw.

Noah, who'd been quietly standing to one side, cleared his throat. "Jazz, as your friend, I must warn you, withholding information will only exacerbate the whole situation." He adjusted the black elastic on his glasses as he tried to look older than his fourteen years.

Jazz frowned at him. "Speak English, Noah."

He paused, thinking. "I mean to say, if you zip your lip, Matt will flip." He smiled, satisfied at his translation.

Speechless, Jazz stared back at Noah, as though astonished at his newest vocabulary additions.

"Noah's been listening to some hip hop," Matt explained. "But he's right. You'd better tell us what happened."

Jazz still hesitated, then reluctantly nodded her head. "Okay. You asked for it. I was shooting a few hoops at the schoolyard when these *kids* showed up and began shouting comments from the sidelines. You know, trash talkin', but it started getting to me. Finally, I told the guy if he was so hot, to come and have a quick game of pickup with me. He started laughing and walked out onto the court, showing off for his girlfriend who was sitting in the shade with the rest of the kids. Anyway, to cut a long story short, as soon as the guy got hold of the ball, he wouldn't give it back. He told me to go home and play with my dolls and leave basketball to the men."

She shook her head. "You know I couldn't take that,

Matt. I went ballistic. I ran toward him and jumped, trying to grab the ball out of his big, meaty paws, but the guy strong-armed me and I ended up flat on my face. That's when I scraped my knee."

Jazz paused and Matt could sense she was holding something back. "You know who this guy was?" His voice was very calm.

She glanced from Free Throw to Matt then sighed heavily. "It was Beal," she said reluctantly.

"I knew it!" Matt exploded. "That rotten, no good . . ."

"Whoa, hold on a minute, Matt. No sense getting bent out of shape. Let's think about this a moment." Free Throw quickly rolled his chair forward, as though riding in on a white charger to Jazz's defence.

Matt stopped his tirade. "Okay, okay, I guess you're right. It's just when it comes to spreading bad news, Beal is the North American distributor." He paced around the court, cursing to himself and anyone else in earshot.

"We're not going to let him get away with this, are we?" Jazz asked. "We should go right down there and get my, I mean *your* ball back."

Matt frowned dubiously. "Uh, yeah, sure. Any idea how?"

A sly grin spread across Jazz's face. "Hey, I'm getting a great idea. I know what we should do. We'll march down there and challenge his butt to a game. He'd have to accept because his skinny girlfriend is there and he'd look like a chicken if he didn't play us."

Matt seemed doubtful. "Jazz, you have to rest that leg. Tomorrow we're playing the Mean Machine and we're already one player short. We'll go get the ball back." He nodded at Noah and Free Throw. "Let's go, guys. Beal's about to find out a whole new meaning for the term *triple threat*."

Free Throw shook his head. "I'm not sure your brain is running on all three cylinders, but count me in." He high-fived Matt. "No way I'm letting you face that goon alone."

Noah stuck his chin out. "As Athos, Porthos, and Aramis, The Three Musketeers, would say: 'All for one, and one for all!' I am ready to gird my loins and enter the fray with my basketball brothers."

Jazz, Matt, and Free Throw stopped and stared at him.

Noah cleared his throat and smiled sheepishly. "Count me in, guys."

"All right, Tiger!" Matt grinned at the tall youth. "You know the really weird part is I'm starting to understand Noah-ese and it's a little frightening." He started toward the path. "Let's go!"

Precious, who loved a good scrap, barked excitedly in agreement.

Jazz cleared her throat. "Uh, there's something else you should know, Matt . . ."

"You can watch if you want, Jazz, but no playing on

that leg. Tell me the rest when we get there." He was already anticipating that first basket and didn't want to wait for her.

★ ★ ★

As they approached the schoolyard, Matt saw Beal and his friends lounging under the trees that ran along the far side of the basketball court. He sometimes wondered what life was like for Beal. He could understand why the guy was so bitter and such a hard case, but it was still no reason to act the way he did. Beal knew he was being a jerk, and apparently saw nothing wrong with it.

Matt remembered when he'd been on the receiving end of some grim comment directed at him because he was an Indian. The easy way would have been to become angry and bitter and then pound the guy into the ground, which was how Beal handled things. Matt's mom had taught him a different way. She'd always told him, "You don't fight fire with fire, you fight fire with water." Cool things down, don't heat them up.

This approach had saved Matt a number of times. After all, fighting someone because his skin was a different colour was pretty stupid. There were a lot of important things in life worth fighting over. The trick was figuring out which were the important ones and which weren't. Beal's problem was he hadn't figured out which were the important things.

Matt headed straight for Beal. He wasn't going to fight, but he was still furious at the big bully for shoving Jazz down, not to mention he'd stolen Matt's favourite ball. And as far as Matt was concerned, it was a toss-up which was the worse deed to have done.

"Beal, I think you have something that belongs to me and my sister," he said as calmly as he possibly could under the circumstances.

Beal slowly turned to glare at Matt. "Well lookie here. If it ain't Eagletail, and," he glanced at Free Throw and Noah, who were behind Matt, "you brought re-inforcements. But from the looks of those freaks, I wouldn't count on much help."

Free Throw didn't say anything. Instead, he wheeled up beside Matt. Noah walked over and stood on Matt's other side. Two of Beal's buddies got up and moved to stand with Beal. Matt could feel the tension rising in the air. He knew he couldn't fight Beal. The outcome wouldn't be pretty.

"Here's the deal," he said loud enough so Beal's girlfriend, a startling-looking girl with jet-black hair and artificially white skin, could hear. "We're not here to fight, we're here to play basketball. First team to eight quick points wins, agreed?" He stared at Beal, not blinking. Free Throw began tugging on special thin leather gloves with extra padding in the palms.

Beal scoffed. "Me and my guys against who? You and your band of merry misfits? That ought to be tough.

What's in it for me?" His eyes narrowed suspiciously.

"If you win, you get to keep that very expensive, top flight, practically new basketball. If we win, we get the ball back and you apologize to Jazz for that unnecessary hit you gave her." He waited for Beal's answer.

"*If* we win?" Beal laughed with a strange strangled sound. "You're on, Eagletail. Oh, and to make it a little more even, meet the newest member of the Mean Machine." He jerked his thumb toward the trees.

Matt couldn't believe what he was seeing. Mary Blake stepped out of the shadows and walked across the court. All he could do was stare as his heart did a nosedive into nowhere. Beside him, he could hear Noah gasp, then Free Throw cursed under his breath.

"I decided to play for a winning team, for a change," Mary said with a steely edge to her voice. She stared defiantly at Matt; her pretty mouth set in a hard line. He didn't know what to say to her. He felt like his stomach had suddenly tied itself around his throat and was choking him.

"Mary . . ." he stammered.

"Let's not get sentimental, Matt. We're here to play ball," she said tersely as she put her hands on her hips, signalling their conversation was at an abrupt end.

Beal strolled back to where his girlfriend waited and handed her his black leather jacket. She smiled up at him.

Matt tore his eyes away from Mary and watched

Beal. He was what the girls called good-looking. Personally, Matt couldn't figure out why girls would go for him just because he was tall, muscular, had great hair, and dressed like he owned some trendy clothing store.

"You losers are pathetic," Beal scoffed, showing his incredibly white teeth as he swaggered back toward Matt.

"Come on, Ralph, and you too, Mary." He grinned at the newest teammate on the Mean Machine. "We've got a fast game to win." The three players took their positions on the court.

Matt looked at Free Throw, then Noah. "Come on, guys, we have jerk butt to kick."

Mary stood at centre court. Matt found it hard to bring himself to look at her. It made him feel terrible.

The ball went up and so did Matt. Beal was no match for the Cloud Leaper's spring-loaded legs. He tipped the ball to Free Throw, who only had to touch it with his Velcro-hands and it was home. Matt marvelled for the hundredth time at Free Throw's strength. The guy was amazing.

Free Throw turned toward Beal's basket and snapped a pass to Noah. Ralph had Noah covered. By making a supreme effort, Noah was able to grab the ball before it was intercepted by Beal's teammate. With almost painful slowness, Noah began carefully and precisely dribbling toward the far basket. His concentration was impressive, if not downright annoying.

Mary slid past Noah, who was focused on his dribble. Using a move that was totally against the rules, she suddenly reached out and grabbed Noah's arm in mid-bounce. With her other hand, she slapped the ball over to where Ralph was waiting. Ralph grabbed the ball and passed it to Beal, who sauntered up to the basket and casually tossed it in.

"Mary! I'm appalled!" Noah chided his sister in a stern voice.

Mary ignored him as she ran back to her line.

"No fair, Beal," Matt protested, shaking his head. "That's cheating."

Beal ignored him as he patted Mary on the back. "Way to go, Mary. You're going to fit right in with the Machine." Mary nodded as she took her place alongside Beal. Her face looked like it was carved out of pale, cold marble.

As the ball was inbounded, Beal motioned to his teammates and the three of them moved toward Matt's line. Mary avoided Matt's gaze.

While Matt and Free Throw worked the ball toward the net, Noah ran down the sideline, almost tripping over an untied shoelace as he went. When Matt thought he was close enough for an easy layup, he sent a perfect bounce pass directly to Noah.

Noah grabbed the ball, fumbled, but managed to hold onto it. Gauging the distance, he headed for the waiting hoop. Matt held his breath. Noah stopped, counted two steps, and then went up, his arms lifting the ball at the right angle. He released the ball, sending it straight at the basket.

Straight at the basket rim. The ball clanged against the hoop and bounced back harmlessly. Noah stared at the ball, unable to believe it didn't go in. He silently watched as it rolled across the ground and ended up under a bush near the end of the baseline. The black-haired girl ran to retrieve the ball and flipped it to Beal.

"If that's your best shot, this is going to be even easier than I thought," he snorted.

Beal tossed the ball to Ralph, then cut for the far basket. Ralph dribbled a couple of times and passed the ball back to him.

Beal began moving past Noah. Using all the defensive skills Free Throw had taught him, the lanky astronomer tried to stop Beal, who knocked Noah to the ground with what looked more like a hockey check than a basketball play. Not looking back to see if Noah was okay, Beal drove downcourt and, dodging around Free Throw, went in for a basket. His form was perfect. Matt had to admit the guy had skill in the paint.

The black-haired girl on the sidelines whistled her approval. Matt glanced her way. She was starting to really annoy him.

Free Throw grabbed the ball while Matt helped Noah to his feet. "You all right?" he asked, concerned.

"The only appendage bruised is my tarnished

dignity," Noah said, reverting to Noah-ese.

Matt slapped him on the back. "Let's go rout those villains who besmirched your pride."

The three started downcourt. Free Throw fired a chest pass to Noah, who began dribbling slowly toward the net. He glared at his sister as he carefully moved past her. As Noah turned to send the ball back to Free Throw, who had rolled into a perfect scoring position, Mary sprinted forward, grabbed the back of Free Throw's chair and spun him around.

"Hey, cut it out Mary!" Free Throw protested, as the ball rebounded off the side of his wheelchair.

"You losers should have known you were no match for us," Beal taunted.

Matt grabbed the ball as it bounced across the court. Trying to control his temper, he fired a pass back to Noah. Fortunately, Noah caught it, and together they started toward Beal's basket.

All of a sudden, Beal, Ralph, and Mary all began closing on Noah, yelling as they swooped down toward him. Noah's eyes went wide in terror. He stopped, holding the ball in front of him like a shield. Panicked, Noah threw the ball wildly toward Free Throw who desperately tried to grab it as it sailed over his head. His fingertips almost touched it. Matt ran as hard as he could and managed to grab the ball before it went out of bounds.

"Great save, Matt!" Jazz called from the sidelines.

"Go get 'em, Cloud Leaper!"

Matt turned and looked at the net. Then he started dribbling. Beal's squad was moving directly toward him. He kept the ball in close and his free arm out to ward off the other players. He knew Beal would use dirty play to take the ball. He only needed a couple of more steps, then he'd be in shooting range.

As Matt was about to set up for his jumpshot, he was hit hard from behind and sent flying. Ralph grabbed the wildly bouncing ball and passed it to Beal, who easily went in for a basket.

Matt felt the muscles in his back scream. "If you have to win by cheating, Beal, maybe we need to go over the rules so even you can understand them."

"What a baby! What's the matter, Eagletail? Can't take some real competition?" He laughed and sprinted to the far end of the basketball court.

"Okay, if that's the way you want it." Matt called Free Throw and Noah over to him.

"Apparently, we aren't playing by the rules, which means we don't have to be so polite out there. Together we are a triple threat to reckon with, so let's play by Beal's rules."

Noah and Free Throw nodded and headed back onto the court to receive Matt's inbound ball. Matt tossed the ball to Noah, being careful not to throw a bullet. Noah grabbed the ball and a strange look came over his face. Then he smiled. "Beal's rules! I think I might like that!"

Matt and Free Throw could only stare as Noah began dribbling like they'd never seen anyone dribble before. He bounced the ball high, then took it down a couple of inches off the floor. He bounced it between his legs and then whipped the ball behind his back so it went completely around his body as he moved it toward the net. With a fluid motion that surprised Matt, Noah dodged around Mary, and sent a bounce pass to himself as he zipped past his amazed sister.

"Go get 'em, Tiger!" Matt called and began leaping downcourt in high-flying bounds, ending up directly beneath the basket. Free Throw rocked in his chair until the two small front wheels came completely off the ground and he did a wheelie down the middle of the court. Beal stood and watched the antics, not sure what to do next. Noah scooped the ball to Matt in what looked more like a lacrosse throw than a basketball pass, but Matt snagged the wild pass and sent the ball directly at the net.

Swoosh! Two points!

"Yeeehaa!" Jazz called as she did her crazy-walk victory dance. She was so excited, she threw in a couple of extra moves.

Beal, complaining loudly, grabbed the rebound and fired it at Ralph, who turned, dribbling back toward Matt's basket.

Free Throw headed for the helpless guy, his chair sizzling at mach four. Ralph didn't know how to handle a kid in a wheelchair heading directly at him like a semi-trailer out of control. He stood, open-mouthed, as Free Throw careened past so close, Ralph had to jump back to avoid having his toes run over. Snatching the ball out of the hapless guy's hands, Free Throw turned so sharply he almost tipped the chair on its side.

"Matt, take it home!" he called as he fired an over-head pass to Matt, who was already moving toward the basket. Matt, bouncing the ball almost gracefully, took three long strides and sent a perfect two-pointer through the waiting hoop.

"Hey, that's cheating!" Beal yelled, his face red with fury.

"Could be, but that's four points, Beal!" Matt moved back to his position covering Ralph.

Free Throw waited until Mary was turning to start her drive for the net, then with a yell, he swooped down, bumped Mary on the heels with the wheels of his chair and stole the ball. He turned and rolled home, tossing a perfect basket from at least twenty feet out.

The look on Beal's face was murderous. "You asked for it, Eagletail."

"Six points. Next basket takes it, Beal!" Matt said calmly.

Matt snagged a pass from Free Throw, who contin-ued flying toward Beal's end. Noah was busy pretending to dribble toward the basket with an imaginary ball.

"Hey, how's this for an *air ball!*" he spun the

imaginary ball on his fingertip.

He moved up across from Free Throw. Beal and his team swarmed around them, but Matt, Free Throw, and Noah began passing the ball between themselves in short, snappy passes so it was never with one player more than a couple of seconds. As they passed back and forth, they moved closer and closer to the basket, and Matt could taste victory. It was just one short toss away.

Suddenly, with a roar, Beal shoved Noah backwards, kicked Free Throw's chair, sending it spinning, and went for Matt.

He was totally out of control. Matt tried to deke under his outstretched arm, but Beal chopped down on Matt's shoulders, dropping him to his knees. With a shout of triumph, Beal grabbed the ball, turned, and headed for the waiting basket. With a leap even Matt would have been proud of, he went up, the ball leaving his fingertips in a beautiful arc as it sailed toward the net.

Everyone stopped and watched the ball as it started down toward the waiting hoop. Matt's heart sank as the ball swished through the net.

"And the best team wins again!" Beal laughed victoriously. He high-fived Mary, who grinned back at him. Grabbing the ball before Matt could retrieve it, he waved it in Matt's direction. "I believe this belongs to me, Eagletail."

Beal's ebony-haired girlfriend walked up to him. "I'm bored with this. Let's go get something to eat."

She handed him his jacket.

"I think we're done here." He put his arm around her and then reached out and put his other arm around Mary. Together, they started off the court. Suddenly, he stopped and turned back to Matt. "You'll never beat me again in this life, loser."

Matt watched him walk away. Mary looked back at him and something flickered behind her eyes, but she left with Beal before Matt could say anything.

Jazz bounced over to the three boys, inexplicably happy for some reason Matt couldn't fathom. They'd just lost to Beal — again! And this time it was far worse because Mary had helped.

"You guys were something to see. You played one heck of a game." Jazz smiled at the three ball players. "Noah, what can I say? The word *awesome* comes to mind!" She gave Noah's shoulder a friendly punch. The self-conscious youth blushed furiously.

"But Beal's right. We lost." Matt said dejectedly.

"He wouldn't have won if he was in a regular game," Jazz said matter-of-factly. "He wouldn't be allowed to cheat."

"She's right, Matt, don't be so hard on yourself. If Beal tried any of that stuff, the refs would hang him out to dry," Free Throw said, agreeing with Jazz.

"Yeah, sure." Matt dejectedly watched Mary disappear through the trees with Beal and his gang.

10 THE PLOT THICKENS

Matt felt the ruin of his life was complete. Mary had not only ditched him and the Wildcats, not to mention her best friend Jazz, but had joined the enemy. Even Free Throw couldn't cheer him up. At home, Matt moped around, aimlessly tossing baskets, until finally his mom came out to talk to him.

"Why the long face, Honey Bear?" she asked.

"You know, stuff," he answered evasively. He didn't think he could tell even his mom how much he hurt. It didn't seem grown up at all. She looked at him in that way she had which told him she knew already.

"Okay, I've got some problems, but I can handle them, Mom. I have to figure some stuff out, that's all."

"I know you can handle them, Matt, but I want you to remember I'm always here if you want to talk. Also, I remember something my dad once told me many years ago: Life is like breaking a green colt. Lots of bumps, turns, and crazy spins, but that's what makes the ride so much fun and so rewarding. If you're thrown, you have two simple choices. You get back on and finish the ride or you walk away and try a different colt. And Matt," she smiled at her son, "either way is okay, but you have to make the call. Only you know what's right for you."

She went back inside and Matt thought about what she'd said. It wasn't in him to walk away from a fight. He had always faced his problems, win or lose, and wasn't about to change now. But he'd never had to deal with a girl being involved in the fight before.

He went inside and sat next to Free Throw, who was finishing his notes for tomorrow's game. He'd had to make changes to adjust for losing Mary. She'd been a valuable asset to the team.

"All set?" Matt asked.

"I am, how about you?"

Matt grinned weakly and shrugged, "Go Wildcats!" He cheered with all the enthusiasm he could muster, which didn't turn out to be overwhelming.

Free Throw laughed. "You'll have to do better than that tomorrow or we're in trouble."

★ ★ ★

It took all of Free Throw and Matt's efforts to get the Wildcats in the right frame of mind. They seemed to think Beal and his Mean Machine were unstoppable.

"One thing's for sure," Matt chided his teammates,

"if you go out there with that attitude, we might as well toss in the towel now." He glanced at Free Throw. "A great friend once told me, 'You win in your head first.' We've got to go out there like the winners we are."

Larry and Ron nodded and Jimmy Big Bear high-fived Tony Manyponies.

"That's more like it!" Matt grinned. He noticed Jazz remained pretty quiet. She kept looking over to the Machine's empty bench, waiting for them to make an appearance. With a loud cheer, the Machine suddenly came running through the doors and hit the floor with Beal in the lead. Mary was with them. Matt stood and watched as she warmed up with the rest of the team. It was weird to see her in Machine colours.

"Well, will you get a load of that!" Jimmy said in his usual no nonsense way. "She *is* playing for the enemy. I didn't think she had the guts to show up here against us."

"It's a good thing you came up with all those new plays, Free Throw." Ron said. "Otherwise she'd know exactly what we're going to do."

Matt looked over at him, then at Mary who was busy practising layups, a thought sneaking into the back of his brain.

Jazz was setting out bottles of cold spring water. "You guys are paranoid." She twisted her face into a ghoulish mask. "The Machine's got you spooked."

Nigel had arrived late and only now came out onto the court with Noah dragging behind. "Mere words

can't tell of my disappointment in my own sibling,"
Noah said sadly as he watched his sister warm up on
the court. "Maybe if I'd been a better brother to her, if
I'd only seen the signs . . ."

"Noah, for crying out loud," Free Throw rolled his
eyes. "Don't worry about it. Mary's playing for another
team, that's all."

"It's showtime, guys," Matt interjected, cutting off
the conversation. "We beat the Machine, then on to the
tournament."

The game started fast and Matt decided to use one
of Free Throw's new plays to get the team off to a
good start. It was a variation on a simple give-and-go
play, but used two other players as screens to cover the
high-post receiver until the handoff back to the passer.

"Cory, you and Jazz screen Jimmy. I'll pass," Matt
said, as they set up for the tipoff. He noticed Mary
across the jump circle from him. She avoided his eyes
when he looked at her.

The whistle blew and Cory went up, nudging the
ball to Matt, who grabbed it, dribbling downcourt. He
saw everyone was set up, then sent the ball rocketing to
Jimmy, who had dropped back the second the ball had
left the ref's hand.

The play went like clockwork, right up until the
point when Matt tried to swoop by and take the ball
back from Jimmy before going in for a layup. He'd
made it through his screens, when he ran smack

into two Machine players, big ones. They were exactly where they shouldn't be. Not able to shoot or move, he pivoted and fired the ball to Cory who was on the weak side and had fewer defenders. He wasn't expecting the pass and missed the ball, which was immediately picked up by a Machine player who turned for the Wildcats' basket.

Everyone scrambled, but Beal and his team were fast. Matt found himself pitted against Mary, who was setting a pick for the ball-handler. He should have shoved right by, but couldn't bring himself to use strong-arm tactics on her. Instead, he faked her out then dodged past, reaching the ball-handler a split second too late. The ball was already in the air and arcing toward its target. *Swish*, two points for the Machine.

Matt moved back downcourt without meeting Mary's eyes. He concentrated on the activity around him. Jazz and Cory had a quick little play that Noah and Ron were supposed to help on.

They'd just set it up when, from nowhere, Beal and two of his goons stopped the play by taking Cory, the intended ball-receiver, out in a nasty way. Matt couldn't figure how they knew Cory was going to get the ball.

"The same thing's happening," Tony said, fuming. "They must have ESP."

By halftime, the score wasn't even close.

Nigel headed onto the floor with Cory and Jimmy, a confident smile on his face. "We're here to win, so pass me the ball and I'll show you how it's done," he bragged.

"*If* you're in the open," Cory said.

"And *if* we don't have a better shot," Jimmy added.

But it turned out Nigel did have the best scoring opportunity.

"Nigel, coming at you!" Jimmy called, passing him the ball.

"That's more like it!" Nigel turned for the basket.

He went up from close to the three-point line and Matt held his breath as the ball arced high in the air before heading straight down into the waiting net. "Way to go, Nigel!" he yelled from the sidelines. You had to give the guy credit; he really was a hot shooter.

"In your face, Beal!" Jazz called and whistled loudly with two fingers in her mouth.

The Wildcats pushed harder than they ever had before, but it wasn't enough. The Mean Machine walked away with another win. This was the last game before the tournament on Saturday. With each loss to the Machine, the Wildcats had slipped further in the standings. They still had a chance, even as things stood now, but Matt knew it was a slim one.

"See you guys at practice," Matt called to his teammates as they left. They waved goodbye unenthusiastically. He knew none of them believed there was enough practice in the world for them to be able to beat the Machine. Nigel was busy chatting on his cell as he left and didn't return Matt's wave. Matt shrugged and walked over to where Free Throw waited to be helped into the van.

"You don't seem too upset over today's loss, Point Guard. Is there something you're not sharing?" Free Throw asked suspiciously once he was settled into his seat and buckled up.

"I've got a hunch and I know just the person to help me figure things out," Matt answered cryptically.

Jazz walked up to the waiting boys. "You guys got everything under control?" she asked, tossing her own bag onto the floor of the van.

"Oh, I think we do now," Matt said, watching Jazz.

Jazz looked at him, shook her head, and climbed into the van. When they arrived home, they finished stowing their gear, then met in the family room for a snack. As they were about to start eating the freshly-made pita pockets Matt's mom had waiting, the phone rang.

"Jazz, it's for you, dear," her mother called from upstairs.

Jazz took the call on the extension in the family room. She began talking excitedly into the phone, causing both Matt and Free Throw to stop eating.

"Okay, just calm down," Jazz said. "Tell me again what happened." She listened to the agitated caller on the other end of the phone. "No way! No way! Get out! Great work! I think it's time we busted this case wide open. Come on over. We have to talk." She hung up the phone and turned to face Matt and Free Throw, who were staring at her intently.

"What?" she asked as though nothing out of the ordinary had happened.

"Jazz, after that call, I think we should all have a little meeting, don't you?" Matt suggested to his stepsister.

"I don't know what you mean," Jazz said innocently.

Free Throw, who didn't have a clue what was going on, looked over at Matt. "A meeting? What kind of a meeting? Is this something the coach should sit in on or do you two need a referee instead?"

"Jazz knows what I mean." Matt glanced at his stepsister, who was studiously ignoring him. "Do you want me to get ugly?" he asked, trying to sound tough.

"Matt, you get any uglier and we'll have to put a sack over your head," Jazz said grinning. "Don't worry. We were going to tell you, but we had to wait until we had the goods. We do, and we will, as soon as my spy gets here."

They'd finished eating, including a large tray of freshly-baked assorted cookies, when there was a small knock at the door. Matt pushed four of the cookies to the side of the tray and went to get it.

"I saved you some butterscotch cookies. I know you like them." He stepped back and opened the door wider. Mary walked into the family room.

"Hi guys," she said in a voice that was little more than a whisper. "Sorry about the game today, but . . ."

"But it should be the last time that happens," Jazz finished the sentence for her friend.

"How did you figure it out, Hotshot?" she asked

Matt as he flopped onto the couch.

"Because I'm a freakin' genius, Jazz. Why didn't you let us in on the plan from the beginning instead of making me feel like pond scum all week?" His tone was accusing.

"You missed Mary, huh?" she asked, a knowing smile on her face.

Matt glanced at Mary who was busy eating one of the cookies. "Of course *we* missed her. The Wildcats need players like her."

Jazz held up a finger, shaking her head and making her long, golden hair dance around her head. "Nope, that's not what I asked you. I asked if *you* missed Mary."

Matt felt his face grow red. "Yes, okay, *I* missed Mary. Happy? Now, what's that got to do with your secret master plan?"

"Not a thing. I thought Mary ought to know how you feel about her and this seemed like a good opportunity to get you to 'fess up." Jazz grinned impishly and took a cookie from the plate.

Mary blushed furiously and looked down at her own half-eaten cookie, but Matt could see the small smile tug at her lips.

"Would someone please bring me into the loop?" Free Throw said, looking bewildered.

Matt held his hands up in surrender. "Not me, that's for sure. Which one of you two super-sleuths is going to spill the beans?"

"Let Jazz, she's the one who figured it out in the first place." Mary moved over and sat beside Matt.

"It all started after I noticed the Machine seemed to know our every move," Jazz began. "No one's that good at defence. Mary's the one who actually got my brain moving when she asked you if we were telegraphing our moves somehow," she said to Matt. "I got to thinking if we're not telegraphing on the floor, maybe the Machine knew our plays going in. What if someone had sold us out? It wouldn't matter how many new plays you came up with, Free Throw, the spy would tell the Machine and poof! We're sitting on the losing side of the scoreboard."

She went on. "We decided Beal was the guy to cover because he'd been so smug about winning and besides, he's always had it in for you, Matt. Anyway, when we were shopping for the twins' birthday presents, do you remember we saw Beal going into the park?" Matt and Free Throw both nodded like enthralled children.

"Well, we followed him to see who he'd waved to. We saw the culprit hand over some papers with plays written on them and knew we were right. We had a snake-in-the-grass on the team. The only problem was we couldn't see who the snake was. He was in a car and it drove away right after the handoff." She reached for another cookie. "That's when we decided to come up with Operation Double Agent. Mary and I would pretend to fight, then she'd go to Beal with a story about hating the Wildcats and wanting to join the Machine for revenge on you in particular, Matt." She flashed him a grin. "You're such a handy target. Lots of people can't wait to lay a beating on you! We figured Beal wouldn't turn her down because he knew you liked Mary and it would rip you up to see her playing for the Machine."

Matt squirmed awkwardly. Had it suddenly become warm in here?

Mary patted Matt on the hand. "We had to make everyone believe I'd joined the Machine for real because we still didn't know who the guy was that had sold us out," Mary added. "I'm sorry for making you feel so bad, Matt. I did it for —" she paused, letting her hand rest on his for a second longer than she needed to —"for the team. I couldn't let the Wildcats get cheated. They've worked so hard." She pulled her hand back. "Remember that day in the schoolyard when we went three-on-three? I felt terrible, but I had to prove to Beal I was on his side and that I hated you guys."

She looked at Matt and he saw the pain in her eyes. "It's okay. I understand why you had to do it." He smiled reassuringly at her.

"There's something else you should know," Mary went on awkwardly. "John has a crush on me and he thinks I can play ball." She looked around at anyone but Matt. "I guess I made a good impression on him when he ran into us at the Stampede. He said it was love at first sight and the fact I'm the only girl he's ever met who can actually play decent ball, well, what can I say? I was a hit with him. He's not such a bad guy, once you get to know him," she said, teasingly.

Jazz rolled her eyes. "Yeah, yeah, Attila the Hun falls for Mata Hari. It's the same old, same old. Now, can I get on with my story, for crying out loud?" She forged on. "Okay, by this time Mary's on the bad guys' team and snooping like a mad dog."

Matt looked over at his stepsister and raised an eyebrow.

"It's a figure of speech," she shrugged and went on.

"Well, the whole thing busted wide open this afternoon when Beal got a phone call from the informer. Mary overheard them discussing where to meet to hand over the next bunch of plays for the game on Saturday. The genius girl made up some excuse to borrow Beal's phone and star-sixty-nined the last caller." She looked over at her friend sympathetically. "You can't imagine how poor Mary felt when she recognized the caller's phone number. She almost fell over when it turned out to be someone she cared about, a lot, and whom she'd trusted."

Matt felt his stomach tighten. Mary cared about some other guy?

"I felt so betrayed," Mary said, her voice choked with emotion.

Matt felt a little choked also.

Finally, he couldn't stand it anymore. If he had a

rival for Mary, even one who'd betrayed her, he had to know. "Okay, enough suspense, who's the snake in the grass, low-life, back-stabbing . . ."

Jazz stared at him, waiting a moment before speaking. Matt was sure she was drawing this out on purpose. "It's . . ." Jazz looked around, "Nigel Blake."

Matt felt his stomach unclench. "It's not a boyfriend, it's her *brother?*"

"Boyfriend? Where'd you get that idea?" Jazz asked, her brows furrowed, but she had a twinkle in her eye.

"Why didn't you let us in on this?" Matt asked.

Jazz grinned mischievously. "And miss out on all this fun? No way."

"The problem is, what do we do about it now that we know?" Free Throw rubbed his hands together. "I, for one, can think of a couple of things I'd like to do, but they're illegal in Canada as well as in forty-eight states." He scanned the assembled group. "Any ideas?"

Everyone looked thoughtful, but no one had any brilliant suggestions. Matt suddenly realized something grim.

"There's one more thing. No matter what we come up with, you'll have to stay with the Machine, Mary, or they might smell a rat." He saw her swallow.

"I know. But as long as the right team wins, I don't mind, really."

Her words were brave, but Matt heard the tremor in her voice. "Don't worry," he smiled warmly at her.

"When it comes time to engrave our names on the winning trophy, I'll make sure they spell *Mary Blake* correctly." Mary returned his smile. It was small and very tentative, but he felt like a twenty-ton weight had been lifted off his heart.

Matt stood up and paced. "This is going to take something particularly tricky." His face was screwed up in concentration, then he stopped. "Wait a minute," he said slowly, then nodded his head. "I think I have the perfect plan! It's so simple, it's got to work!" He motioned for them to gather around.

"This is what we're going to do . . ."

11 THE MOST IMPORTANT GAME ISN'T ALWAYS PLAYED ON THE COURT

"Are you sure everyone knows the signals?" Matt asked for the hundredth time.

"Relax, Point Guard. The Wildcats know what they're doing," Free Throw said calmly. "I have those guys humming like a well-oiled machine. No worries."

Matt nodded. He had to try and relax. He was supposed to show these guys how to be cool under fire and here he was practically vibrating. He looked around at Calgary's huge Adams Sports Centre auditorium where the round robin tournament was being held. The place was packed. There were two full-size basketball courts and they'd both been busy all day. Two of the elimination rounds had already been played. The Wildcats had won against the Okotoks Vikings and the Calgary Cowboys. Both teams had played great and fought well.

Matt had tried to find out how Mary was doing, but everyone was too busy and too frantic. They were now waiting to find out whom they played in the final round. It was still possible the Mean Machine, who had won their first round and were now finishing their second, would be eliminated from play. Then the Wildcats would face another, less brutal team for the championship. Stranger things had happened.

Matt could see Noah's tall frame moving through the crowd toward him and Free Throw. Somehow, he didn't look as gangly as he did when they'd first started showing him which end of a basketball was up. His stride seemed more confident. When it came right down to it, Matt decided he liked this astronomy geek.

"Hey, guess what I heard?" Noah began, grinning.

Matt and Free Throw stopped, amazed.

"What did you say?" Matt asked.

Noah looked at them. "Come on, guys. You're kidding, right?"

At that moment, Jazz walked up, her long blond braid swinging jauntily behind her. "Hi, did Noah tell you the news?"

"He was going to, but we *didn't* need a translator, so we couldn't understand him," Matt explained.

Jazz frowned at Matt and shook her head. "You're strange, you do know that, right?"

"Okay, Noah, out with it," Free Throw prompted.

"Moments ago, I watched my sister's *temporary* team win. We play the Mean Machine in an hour."

Matt knew how much it had hurt Noah to find out about Nigel. The only thing that had kept him going was knowing what his sister had done for the Wildcats.

Mary was a sister anyone could be proud of. Not that Matt wasn't proud of his own sister. Jazz had been great through this whole deal, especially after he and Free Throw had convinced her *not* to stuff Nigel into a basketball net headfirst. In fact, she'd suggested a couple of plays, which Free Throw was going to use.

Matt saw the rest of the Wildcats walking toward them. Nigel was nowhere to be seen.

"Did you hear?" Jimmy asked.

"You bet — we get to get Beal. He's in for a real surprise when he plays us today." Matt tried to sound confident.

Jimmy nodded his head. "And so is a certain lowlife creep who sold us out. No offence, Noah." He slapped Noah so hard on the back that his glasses slid down to the end of his nose.

"No offence taken." Noah shoved his glasses back up to where they belonged.

Matt checked the clock. "We've got a little time. Let's meet back here in half an hour, ready to win this tournament." He left to find Mary. This game was going to be hard for her and he wanted to wish her luck. Matt had been surprised at how much Beal was playing his only female teammate. Maybe the guy could spot talent when he saw it, Matt thought, remembering how quick on her feet Mary was and what a great touch she had with the ball. She was a natural!

Spotting Mary in the juice line, Matt deked in

behind her. "Can I talk to you?"

"Sure. Let me get my drink and we can go outside." She finished paying the concession operator and together they made their way through the crowd. Once outside, they found a bench under a tall tree and sat in the shade, relaxing.

Matt didn't know how to begin. "Uh, Mary, actually, I wanted to . . . to wish you luck. No matter who wins, we all gave our best, and some," he looked at her, "more than others."

Her eyes met his. "You know I'd do anything for the Wildcats, Matt."

"And I'd do anything for you, Mary," Matt said, without thinking. "I mean, you know," he smiled sheepishly at her.

"I know." She wiggled a little closer and they sat together in companionable silence, watching the birds swoop and dive over the small lake that was adjacent to the sports complex. Matt could have sat there all day and into the night, but duty called.

"I guess we'd better head back," he said reluctantly.

"We can continue this conversation later," Mary suggested.

With a confidence he didn't know he had, Matt took her hand and held on as they walked back to the building. It didn't get any better than this.

★ ★ ★

The Wildcats were gathered around their bench when Matt walked in. Nigel was there, looking very pleased with himself.

"Hi guys, everyone ready?" Matt asked with an enthusiastic grin. "Today, we bag the big one!" Nigel looked at him questioningly.

"The championship, trophy, prize, you know, the reason we all showed up," Matt explained.

"Oh, right," Nigel said. "I forgot. We're going to beat the Machine today, unlike every other time we've played them."

"Not every time," Matt corrected. "Just lately." He decided to change subject before he said something to alert Nigel they were on to his tricks.

"I wanted you guys to know, win or lose, this has been quite a summer." He took in each of their happy faces. They deserved to win; they'd earned it. "Now let's go show these rookies how to play the game of games!"

Matt squared off against Beal. "Nice day for a little game of pickup, don't you think, Beal?" he said conversationally.

Beal seemed confused by this, not having expected it at all.

"I'd say it was a good day to wipe the floor with some wimps, if that's what you mean, Eagletail," he grinned at Matt, showing his white teeth.

Matt noticed one of the front teeth had a chip off the end. It made a tiny whistle when Beal talked.

The ball went up and Cory launched into their first play of the game. He tapped the ball to Larry Chang, who dribbled toward the side of the court. The Machine players moved to cover him. In the meantime, the 'Cats had set themselves up so they could all break and run to pre-set spots for the follow-up play.

Nigel knew this play, it was supposed to go from Larry to Matt, then back to Cory, who would have moved into the open where he could go in for an easy layup. Matt could already see the extra Machine men moving toward Cory.

"Go 'Cats!" he called, and immediately the ball came whizzing over to Matt who zipped a quick chest pass to Jazz, who had hung back. She turned, cut around her man, and went for the net.

The Machine players were all out of position, and Jazz had no traffic to go through before she tossed the first basket of the game. Her crazy walk had an extra wiggle in it as she danced past Beal. "That's two for us and none for you!"

Beal shot Nigel a questioning look, but Nigel ignored him.

The next scoring opportunity came when Matt, who was supposed to be the *give* player in a quick give-and-go between himself and Ron, went with the new game plan where he was the *go* guy instead. Ron set a pick and Matt dodged around him, then went up for beautiful jumpshot.

Nothing but net!

As the game progressed, Beal and his team were left further and further behind as Free Throw's new endings to old plays paid off. The Wildcats' new game strategy, which Nigel had been left out of, was working beautifully. The Machine was being run all over the court.

"If they'd play an honest game, instead of always trying to use the stuff Nigel gave them, we might not have the great lead we do," Matt said, wiping his forehead with a towel.

"Yeah, but they still can't believe we're smart enough to be onto them. They think we're screwing up the plays because we're no good at this game." Free Throw laughed. "They have no idea how good we are!"

By three-quarter time, Beal was furious and his team was ten points behind. Matt saw him talking to his players at their bench. When they came back out onto the floor, Mary came with them. Matt didn't like the smugness on Beal's face. He was up to something and Matt knew it.

"I thought your little girlfriend ought to have a shot at you too, Eagletail." Beal had a glint in his eye.

"Cory, you and Jimmy watch Mary. Something funny is going on." Matt nodded at Jazz and Tony. They were going to start a play with a twist that should drive Beal crazy. It would start at the foul line and was a variation on the up-formation, a pass-and-screen-away offence which involved Matt passing to Jazz, who was playing left wing. He would then set a screen away from the ball and Tony was supposed to use this screen to cut across the middle and receive the pass from Jazz. Tony would then turn and shoot. Simple — except, instead of passing to Tony, Jazz would now pass to Matt, who would have an open jumpshot.

The play went great. The Machine players expected the ball to be passed to Tony and swarmed all over him. Matt had no trouble dumping in a beautiful two-pointer. The ball had barely dropped into the basket when he heard a commotion behind him on the court. He turned to see Cory bending over Mary, who was flat on her back on the floor and not moving. Beal was walking away from her.

Suddenly, with a tremendous roar, Noah came charging off the bench and spun Beal around. "You did that on purpose, you big bully. I saw you stick out your foot and shove her down. She's on the same freakin' team as you, or are you so stupid you forgot that little detail?" Noah yelled in Beal's face. He no longer looked like an astronomy nerd, but like an outraged big brother who was about to defend his little sister with his fists.

Matt saw Beal's eyes glaze over. "You little . . ." Beal clenched his own fist.

Matt grabbed his arm before he could bring it up. "Hold on. What happened?"

"This nematode here flattened my sister on purpose. I saw him," Noah said angrily.

"You're crazy, you weirdo. She tripped and fell," Beal said defensively.

Matt knew how accidents had a way of happening around Beal. He turned to where Cory was helping Mary to her feet.

"Are you okay, Mary?"

"I had the wind knocked out of me but I'll be fine." She grimaced, then smiled at him, but Matt saw how white her face was.

"Mary, you've got to believe me. I didn't want this to have to happen but . . ." Beal's voice trailed off as the ref moved in to check Mary.

Matt turned back to Beal. His voice was low and deadly. "If you ever pull any of that stuff again, I'll personally arrange it so you're tossed off the court. Two can play at your game, Beal, and I make a great victim. The refs will take one look at a big strong goon like you and a short, light guy like me and guess who'll get the free throw? Pick up enough fouls and you'll be riding the pine permanently. No one wants to play with a liability who gets fouled out game after game."

Beal, his fists still clenched, turned and strode away, but Matt had seen the hesitation in his eyes. He'd been taken aback by the conviction in Matt's voice. Mary went to sit on the bench to recover, but it wasn't with the Machine. She sat sheltered between Free Throw and Jazz with the Wildcats where she belonged.

The next substitutions saw Noah and Nigel on the

floor together. Nigel, who was not in the best position, yelled at Larry to pass the ball to him. Larry, who was covered, had no choice and passed the ball to Nigel. Suddenly, with lightning speed, Noah cut in on his brother, grabbed the ball, and screamed to the other end of the court. He manoeuvred through the Machine players like they were nailed to the floor. His dribbling was fantastic as he moved the ball from one hand to the other, always keeping it away from danger, then sliding it behind his back and under one leg then the other. He was laughing as he jumped to an incredible height and fired from inside the three-point line. He never even watched it go in, he was that sure it was good.

The crowd jumped to its feet and cheered. Noah and his unbelievable shot was the hero of the game. He waved and bowed. Matt, standing on the sidelines, clapped right along with everyone else. That basket had been the stuff of legends! Nigel was so stunned, he forgot to get angry with his brother.

There was time left for only one play. The Wildcats had an unbeatable lead as Matt took the handoff from Jimmy. He started down the court, then saw Beal right in front of him. Beal looked like he was going to mow Matt down in a big way. Matt glanced at Free Throw, who gave the thumbs-up.

Matt turned back to Beal, and casually tossed him the basketball. Beal caught the ball and stood on the court, holding it like he wasn't sure what this strange thing was. Then he came to his senses and started for the Wildcats' basket. As he went up for the only slam-dunk shot of the game, the final buzzer sounded. The basket was good and the Machine racked up two more points, but it wasn't nearly enough.

Wildcats 94, Mean Machine 36!

The crowd didn't seem to notice Beal's shot, but was already yelling and whistling. There were balloons dropping from the ceiling and fans cheering. Matt waved to his family in the stands and they all waved back. Precious howled his congratulations.

Matt walked over to the bench and before he could say anything, Mary jumped up and hugged him enthusiastically. "We did it!"

"Nice touch, Point Guard." Free Throw nodded in Beal's direction. "Makes me wish I'd thought of it."

"Looks like we're going to take home a little well-earned loot," Matt reminded the 'Cats as they congratulated each other and poured water over any head within reach.

"Way to go, Hotshot!" Jazz exclaimed as she linked arms with Matt and swung him around. "I knew we'd do it." She released Matt and headed for Free Throw who was being slapped on the back by Cory. Matt was astonished as he watched his stepsister hug their proud coach around the neck. He couldn't be sure, but he thought he saw Free Throw blush!

"This has been a too-cool summer, Cloud Leaper.

Thanks for inviting us to join," Jimmy Big Bear said, beaming.

"Anytime you need help, give us a call," Tony Manyponies added, snapping Matt on the leg with the corner of his towel.

Larry and Ron had joined Jazz, who was teaching them how to do the crazy wiggle-walk she always did after scoring a basket. Matt shook his head at his strangely gyrating teammates and walked over to where Noah was watching the festivities. "You know, Noah, you might want to trade that telescope of yours in on a Spalding basketball. You were awesome out there!" He smiled at Noah as the young athlete adjusted the black strap on his glasses.

"Upon reflection, it does give one pause for thought and mayhap, personal goal re-evaluation," he said in Noah-ese, then winked and high-fived Matt. "Besides, the girls really go for us jocks!"

As everyone gathered their belongings and prepared to go home to change for the victory banquet, Matt noticed Nigel standing alone at the far end of the bench. His face was a mixture of controlled anger and resignation.

Matt went to pick up his own gear, which was on the floor next to Nigel's. "Quite a game. It goes to show what you can do when everyone pulls together for the team."

Nigel didn't reply, instead he viciously jammed his water bottle into his gym bag.

"You know the really great part?" Matt asked, ignoring Nigel's show of anger. "We won because we really are the best team here. The Mean Machine can try all the dirty tricks in the book, but the good guys — that's us — can still beat them in a fair fight."

Nigel whirled on him, his face scarlet. "You know something, Eagletail? I'm really glad I'm finished with this loser league," he spat through gritted teeth. "I sure won't be back next year. This has been nothing but a huge waste of my time."

His extreme reaction made Matt wonder if perhaps, just perhaps, Nigel's conscience was bothering him a little.

"It's too bad you feel that way, Nigel. The rest of us had a real blast and we *will* be back next year." Matt grabbed his gym bag, and without a backward glance, went to join his team.

★ ★ ★

The banquet was a lot of fun. The Wildcats were all measured for their new sneakers and the names of their favourite players noted for the jerseys. Everyone laughed when Noah asked for a size larger so his would fit him next year when he played for the Wildcats again. Free Throw was eagerly looking forward to his pair of sneakers and Matt had promised to mail both the jersey and the shoes as soon as they came in. Jazz thought they should come up with better uniforms next year, maybe something in red-and-white stripes. The guys had groaned when she'd told them to leave the details to her.

Matt insisted Mary Blake be counted as a Wildcat player and the rest of the team had supported him. He was rewarded for his fairness when she sat next to him at dinner.

The Mean Machine had attended and were as loud and obnoxious as ever.

As they listened to the speeches, Matt glanced around the banquet room. Suddenly, his eyes locked with John Beal's. Matt saw the usual arrogance in his eyes, but he thought he saw something else. He could have sworn he saw a flicker of doubt cross Beal's face. Maybe he knew the next time they faced each other on the basketball court, Matt was going to be tougher to beat.

Matt nodded his head slightly, then smiled confidently. Heck, he was going to be a *lot* tougher to beat. Everyone was wise to Beal's antics and Matt doubted anyone would put up with his bullying anymore.

The congratulations went on late into the night. Noah, with his fabulous shot, was voted the most valuable player of the game and he glowed under the praise. By the time the party broke up, it had been decided they would all be back next year to defend their new championship title.

★ ★ ★

The next day, Free Throw was busy packing when Matt came into their room. "Hey, I've noticed the twins haven't been pestering you lately. Did you finally get tired of them hanging on your every word?"

"As a matter of fact, I've been replaced. A new boy moved in down the road and he is apparently a lot more interesting than I am. My poor jilted heart may never recover from those two fickle Canadian girls." He smiled at Matt.

"I think you have one Canadian girl who won't be fickle." Matt noticed the picture of Jazz in a new frame sitting on top of a pile of Free Throw's clothes.

"Yeah, well, we've become good friends." Free Throw tried to be nonchalant, but Matt saw the flush creep up his face. "As soon as I'm on that plane, I bet Cory will be right back at the top of her list. You know how that goes. Out of sight, out of mind."

"Maybe, but you never know with Jazz."

Matt sat on the edge of his bed. "I talked to Mary on the phone and found out what was going on with Nigel. It seems he took serious offence at some of the comments I made about him. He thought I was an idiot for not acknowledging him as the obvious leader of the team since he was such a great player and was on that first-rate team in Calgary."

Matt held his hands up.

"His words, not mine," he continued. "I guess when we played against Beal the first time, Nigel really impressed him with his basketball expertise and Beal told him so. That was exactly what Nigel wanted to hear and before you could say *dirty play,* those two had come up with a way of ensuring the Wildcats lost. Nigel didn't worry about losing because this whole summer league was a joke to him anyway. He only played in it because he never got accepted to some fancy basketball camp in the States."

"I wonder what his chances of going to that camp will be when word gets around about what really happened?" Free Throw mused as he stuffed a dirty T-shirt into his duffel bag.

"Who knows? Me, I don't care. As far as I'm concerned, things couldn't have worked out better. Our team won, thanks to the absolutely fabulous plays our coach came up with," Matt tossed another dirty shirt at his friend. "You do know I plan on using some of those plays next season when I play for the Bandits again?"

Free Throw nodded. "Help yourself."

"And," Matt went on, "I have a great new friend in Noah, who's going to try out for the school team, by the way." He took a deep breath, "Then there's Mary."

"I'd say from the way you two were making cow eyes at each other at the banquet, it's pretty obvious how you feel about her." Free Throw made smooching noises with his lips.

Matt ignored the tease and cleared his throat. "I've learned a lot this summer and I don't just mean how to play wicked basketball." He looked at Free Throw and knew they were always going to be best friends. "I'm going to miss you, John."

Free Throw stopped packing. "Hey, I'm never more than a cheap Internet provider away, Point Guard. We can be Facebook friends — that way we can keep up with every second of each other's lives." His face became serious as he wheeled over to where Matt sat on the edge of his bed.

"Matt, friends like us don't let a little geography get us down. Next year, you can come and visit me in San Francisco and we'll go watch the NBA finals together. What do you say? It's something to think about."

"And get a chance to watch real pros play live with maybe courtside tickets we could share and a free tour guide for all the high spots? Gee, that's a tough one, Free Throw. I'll have to think about that." He gave his best friend a gentle punch on the arm. "Okay, I've thought about it and you're on. But, we'd better start planning what we're going to do now, because I'll have to squeeze a week of shopping in so I can bring souvenirs home for my *typical Canadian family*. And something special for Mary."

Free Throw raised his eyebrows and Matt laughed.

Next year was shaping up to be a lot of fun already!

MORE SPORTS, MORE ACTION
www.lorimer.ca

CHECK OUT THESE OTHER BASKETBALL STORIES FROM LORIMER'S SPORTS STORIES SERIES:

Camp All-Star
by Michael Coldwell

Jeff's been invited to an elite basketball camp, and he's looking forward to some serious on-court action for two weeks straight — but Chip, his completely unserious new roommate, seems to have other ideas…

Fast Break
by Michael Coldwell

Meeting people in a new town is hard. So when Jeff runs into a group of guys who love basketball as much as he does, he makes sure to stick with them when school starts. But at school, he finds out what they're really like…

Free Throw
by Jacqueline Guest

When his mother remarries, suddenly everything changes for Matt: new school, new father, five annoying new sisters, and even a smelly new dog. Worst of all, if he wants to play basketball again, he'll have to play with his old team's worst enemies.

Home Court Advantage
by Sandra Diersch

Life as a foster child can be tough — so Debbie has learned to be tough back, both at home and on the court. But when a nice couple decides to adopt her, Debbie suddenly isn't so sure of herself — and her new teammates aren't so sure about her either.

Nothing But Net
by Michael Coldwell

Playing in an out-of-town tournament can be rough, especially when you know you're the worst team on the court. But when you've got nothing to lose and a wild man like Chip Carson on your side, anything can happen...

Out of Bounds
by Sylvia Gunnery

As if it isn't bad enough that Jay's family home has been destroyed by fire, Jay has to switch schools — which means he has to choose between playing for the enemy, and not playing basketball at all. And he can't decide which is worse.

Personal Best
by Sylvia Gunnery

Jay finally gets to go to Basketball Nova Scotia Summer Camp, and he even gets to stay in a real dorm with his best friend, Mike. But Mike's older brother is also there, and he's not exactly acting like a good coach or a good big brother... .

Queen of the Court
by Michele Martin Bossley

Kallana's father has suddenly decided that joining the basketball team will be a "character-building" experience for her. But she can't dribble, she can't sink a basket, and worst of all, she will have to wear one of those hideous uniforms...

Rebound
by Adrienne Mercer

C.J.'s just been made captain of the basketball team — but her teammate, Debi, seems determined to make C.J. miserable. Then C.J. wakes up one morning barely able to stand up. How can she show Debi up when she can't even make it onto the court?

Slam Dunk
by Steven Barwin & Gabriel David Tick

The Raptors are going co-ed — which means that for the first time ever, there will be *girls* on the team. Mason's willing to see what these girls can do, but the other guys on the team aren't so sure about this...

Fadeaway
by Steven Barwin

Renna's the captain of her basketball team, and is known to run a tight ship. But then a new girl from a rival team joins. Suddenly, Renna's being left out and picked on by her own teammates. Can she face this bullying and win her team back before it goes too far?